The *Shell Collector's* Daughter

A NOVELLA

BETH WISEMAN

The Shell Collector's Daughter

Copyright 2017 Beth Wiseman
Published by Beth Wiseman in Fayetteville, Texas

Cover design: Beth Wiseman
Interior design: Caitlin Greer

To Janet Murphy

"People tell me that I'm special. I don't see it that way. I'm just different."

~ Carianna Marie Sparks

Prologue

Carianna sat across the table from God, the way she'd done every Thursday for as long as she could remember. In the backyard of her father's shop, there was an oak tree with limbs that were hundreds of years old—three hundred and twelve God had told her. Protective branches formed a dome over Carianna's head, even though no protection was needed on Thursdays.

Her father's shop was far enough away from the beach that Carianna couldn't hear the breaking of the waves, but it was close enough to inhale the briny smells of the ocean. A perfect breeze swirled amid the branches of the old tree as Carianna took a sip of her raspberry tea. She loved living on Mustang Island, and she loved these visits with God.

"I'm sending someone into your life, Carianna," God said as He lifted His blue cup to His lips. "A man of My choosing, a person to be with you for the rest of your days on Earth."

Carianna frowned as her stomach clenched. "I have my father for that." She stared at God, and without knowing why or how, Carianna knew He was perfect. *Perfect love.* A smile replaced her sour expression. "And I have You."

Her friend set His cup on the worn wooden table, and He folded one hand on top of the other. God's hands were wrinkled, like her father's, and God's gray hair swept sideways in wiry wisps to one side of His tanned face. A face filled with connecting lines, spidery and deep. She believed God to be older than her father, but it was hard to know for sure.

"Yes, Carianna, you have your father here on earth, and you have Me as your heavenly Father. But I'm talking about a different kind of man. This man will love you in a way that will be new and unfamiliar to you."

Carianna tipped her head to one side, pushing back long strands of brown hair that blew in front of her face. "Do I know this man?"

God shook his head. "No. Not yet. But you will feel like you know him the moment you meet him. He is a few years older than you, but as you learn of him, just know that I am always with you, so there is no need to be afraid."

Carianna's heart pounded against her chest. She was twenty-six years old, and even though God said there was no need for fear, her breath caught in her throat. "You mean like a boyfriend?" she finally asked.

God smiled. "Yes, Carianna, that's what I mean."

She shook her head as she pressed a hand to her chest. "I don't think I like this idea."

The Lord reached over and touched Carianna's free hand, and the feel of His touch reassured her that all would be well. God's perfect love was never wrong. Carianna was sure of that.

And yet, fear wrapped around her like a serpent, squeezing the life out of her.

Chapter One

Dominic dropped his flip-flops in the sand, lifted his camera, and zoomed in on the seagulls' overhead. He took several shots before he put the lens caps back on and lowered the camera and strap against his chest. His jeans kept the brisk, fall wind from sweeping through his legs, but with only a T-shirt on, his arms pimpled from the cool breeze. Next trip out to San Jose Island, he'd wear a long-sleeved shirt and consider his tennis shoes.

He slipped his feet back into his shoes and took a few steps in the moist sand. As one foot slid sideways against the slick rubber, he kicked off the Nikes again. After he'd rolled up his jeans enough to keep them out of the sand, he picked up the sandals and decided to brave the cool weather barefoot, the moisture molding between his toes like shallow quicksand. Dominic glanced over his shoulder at the ferry leaving in the distance. Only a few people had chosen to venture from Port Aransas to San Jose Island this early in the morning. The sun wasn't even round on the horizon yet, but even though it was daybreak and he'd yawned a lot during the five minute boat ride, he'd gotten some fantastic shots of the sunrise. But now it was time to get to work. San Jose Island was listed as one of the top ten places in the United States for shell collecting. And those in the know had told him to arrive early this morning. He'd missed the first ferry at six-thirty, but caught the next one at seven.

He looked down at the ground and bent over slightly as his camera swayed to and froe, his eyes searching for the shells that he'd heard about. Within a few seconds, he spotted a perfect starfish, glanced at the incoming tide, then snatched it up before a wave swooshed past his ankles, leaving another round of treasures as it receded. After he inspected the sandy earth around him, he lifted his eyes and scanned his surroundings. Only a handful of people strolled the waterline as the sun lifted above the clouds, blending powder puffs of white with the rising orange arc in the sky. A woman he hadn't noticed before glided toward him, as if she was taking steps on a moving walkway at an airport, her strides long and steady. Her gray cap stretched over her ears as loose strands of long brown hair aimlessly danced in the wind. She wore a long-sleeved white shirt with brown stripes, and her blue jeans drug in the sand as she walked in a pair of dark brown Crocs. But it was her eyes that captured Dominic's, hazel orbs guarded by thick lashes that swept against high cheekbones, dimpled on either side of a delicate mouth. She stopped a few feet in front of him, but any hint of a smile Dominic thought he saw seconds ago was replaced with an unreadable expression.

Dominic's knees went weak, something he couldn't recall happening before. This woman was the most gorgeous creature he'd ever seen, and he was drawn to her in a way he couldn't explain. He glanced at her left hand, surprised there wasn't a ring. But this beauty surely had a boyfriend, at the very least. She eased a backpack off her shoulders and gently set it in the sand, then took another step closer to Dominic.

"How old are you?" She tilted her head to one side as she brushed a strand of hair from across her face.

It seemed an odd thing to ask, but Dominic cleared his throat and found his voice. "Twenty-nine." *And you are gorgeous*. She was a small woman with dainty features, but wore no makeup, not even a gloss on her full lips. Her eyebrows weren't manicured like a lot of women, and her nails and toes were unpolished.

"That makes you a few years older than me." She took an exaggerated step backward, almost tripping over her backpack as she scowled. "Three years older to be exact."

"Um…if you say so, okay." He stared at her for a few moments, but she lowered her gaze and kept her eyes cast downward, folding her hands in front of her.

She finally looked up at him and scratched her chin with one finger. "I'm Carianna Marie Sparks."

She spoke softly, and Dominic smiled. "Hello, Carianna Marie Sparks." He decided to follow suit as he boldly took a step forward. "I'm Dominic Wayne Bennett."

Carianna's doe eyes widened with a true deer-in-the-headlight look, and Dominic feared she might take off running down the beach at any moment. But she slowly took a step toward him, her eyes fusing with his.

"Why are you sad?" Her eyebrows met in a frown as she puckered her lips like a child might.

Dominic's stomach lurched. Even during all the traveling he'd done recently, he still couldn't hide the void in his life. "My mom died three months ago." He couldn't believe he was telling a perfect stranger this news.

"Do you have a father?" The tiny lines on her forehead creased even more.

Dominic shook his head. "No. He died when I was ten." He paused, lifting one shoulder up before dropping it slowly. "So, it was just me and my mom for a long time, then I went off to college, went to work, and…" He swallowed back the lump in his throat. "I hadn't seen her in a couple of months when she died unexpectedly."

"Why did she die?"

Dominic took his camera from around his neck since it seemed unusually heavy at the moment. He cradled it in his arm. "You mean, *how* did she die?" He went on, assuming that's what she'd meant to say. "She had a heart attack at home. I didn't even know she had a heart problem. Just gone. Just like that." He lowered his head, but looked up when Carianna moved toward him, then she inched even closer. As she cupped his cheek in her hand, she seemed to regard him with somber curiosity. A heady sensation filled Dominic when her lips parted, like she might kiss him, which seemed highly unlikely. But he was certainly going to let her, if she made an attempt. He could feel her breath, and it caused him to hold his as he wondered about the onion bagel he'd eaten on the ferry.

"Don't be sad about your mother," she said softly as she lifted her right hand to Dominic's other cheek. "In heaven, she isn't sick, and she's with your father."

Dominic wanted and needed to believe that, but hearing Carianna say it in her soft, sweet voice caused him to struggle with the growing knot in his throat. "I hope." He spoke in a whisper, anxious to explore this connection engulfing him. He waited for her to close her eyes, to bring her mouth to his. Why else would she be cupping both his cheeks and staring into his eyes? One kiss, even from her, wouldn't ease his suffering, but he longed to escape the pain, if only for a few moments.

No sooner had the thought strolled into his mind and engaged his senses than she lowered her hands and stepped backward. The void over losing his mother resurfaced. But as Carianna moved away from him, hoisted her backpack on her shoulder, and turned to leave, Dominic felt like he would feel this void for the rest of his life if he didn't see her again.

"Wait!" He picked up his flip-flops and jogged toward her, repositioning his camera atop his chest as it slapped against his muscles with each step. But she looked over her shoulder, then picked up the pace, slowly at first, but then she ran as if her life was at stake.

Carianna slowed down after she reached the far end of the island, far enough away that the stranger wouldn't follow her. She leaned over and huffed, trying to catch her breath, before falling to her knees in the sand. As she relaxed her arms, her backpack slid off. She unzipped it, took a peek, and closed it again. She had enough shells for today. Her father would be pleased.

She pulled out a bag of Cheetos and dumped eight into her hand before she stowed the rest in her backpack. Eating them two at a time, she stared the length of the beach at the stranger who looked like a tiny little man from far away. That's how Carianna wanted to keep him—far away. She opened a bottle of water, took eight gulps, then put it back as she shifted her position and folded her legs underneath her in the sand. She would read for a few minutes and hoped that the man, Dominic, would take the next ferry back to from wherever he came. Then she'd make her way down the beach to catch the next boat later.

As she opened her travel book citing the most beautiful destinations for travel in the United States, her eyes kept drifting down the beach. But she turned to page eight and started to read.

∞

Dominic spotted two dolphins on the portside of the ferry as he journeyed back to Mustang Island. He'd long been a fan of Port Aransas, but even more so of Mustang Island. He was glad his editor had sprung for a condo with a view of the beach. He had a week to gather as much information as possible before he was off to another island on the list of 'Best Places to Collect Shells in the United States.' It was a fluff gig, and he was grateful to his editor, Jeanine, for giving him a week. It was more time than necessary, but would allow him some much needed down time also.

He glanced to his right as a man shuffled through a bag of shells he'd collected. The guy wore worn tan slacks, a tattered white T-shirt, and loafers with a hole in the toe. His long gray hair was pulled into a ponytail, and a spidery web of deep wrinkles covered his tanned, weathered face.

"That's quite a haul," Dominic said as the man picked up a really big starfish and studied it.

The guy shrugged, scowling as he placed his find back in the bag. "Ain't like it used to be, that's for sure." He glowered at Dominic, his yellowing teeth gritted. "More and more people keep showing up. A fellow told me San Jose Island is on some list of the best places to collect shells." He huffed. "Could have done without that list. I'm here every Friday, and over the years, the visitors have picked up and the good shells are more scarce." Raising his chin, he said, "Where's your take for the day?"

Dominic held up his one and only starfish, deciding he wouldn't mention that he was a journalist. This fellow looked like the type who had problems with the world, or anyone invading his proclaimed space.

The guy groaned and shook his head before refocusing on his bag of shells. Dominic gazed at the island as it grew smaller in the distance. Even though the island was public and accessible by ferry, there were no modern conveniences, not even a restroom. It was strictly for shell collectors, fishermen, and those choosing a quiet beach away from more populated areas. Or so he'd read. This guy was clearly a local, and the woman he'd met on the beach seemed at home on San Jose Island also.

"There was, uh…" Dominic scratched behind one ear. "…a girl on the beach. A really pretty woman with long brown hair, and I was wondering if—"

"Yeah, that's Carianna, the shell collector's daughter." His attention was back in the bag sifting through his loot again. "She comes here every Friday to collect shells, then takes them back to her father. The old man makes all kinds of stuff out of them, sells them in his shop. You *ain't* the first one to ask about Carianna."

Dominic was scheduled to leave Thursday, but a primal force was niggling and scratching and clawing at him to extend his stay for a day or two so he might see Carianna next Friday.

"Don't be getting no ideas though." The older man studied a large conch shell. "Carianna's father is a force to be reckoned with if he thinks anyone is interested in his daughter."

Dominic bounced when the ferry hit a wave, causing him to clutch the railing next to him. "Surely she's had boyfriends."

"Not a one," the man was quick to say as he eased the shell back into his knapsack. "And it ain't just her father you'd need to watch out for. I don't know a soul on the island who wouldn't protect Carianna with their life, me included." He paused, glared at Dominic for a few moments, and shook his head. "You're under her spell." He chuckled, a deep growling sort of laugh that wasn't pleasant to hear.

"I'm not under anyone's spell." Dominic rolled his eyes. "I spoke with her about two minutes, that's it." He touched his face, where she'd cupped his cheek. Dominic didn't believe in love at first sight. He'd been slow to fall in love in the past, and he'd really only been truly in love once before, in eighth grade. He wasn't sure that even counted.

The old man set his bag beside him, stroked his long gray beard, and looked out over the ocean. "I believe the good Lord created people like Carianna to set an example for the rest of us. She has a simple way about her, but her heart is pure." He turned his attention back to Dominic. "I watched a wild bird come to Carianna when she was just a small girl. Flew right to her, and she pet that bird like a dog." He shook his head. "I'll never forget that. And years later, she was standing outside her old man's shop, and butterflies circled all around her. Strangest thing I've ever seen." He squinted as he pressed his lips together. "Even critters seem to know Carianna is filled with goodness."

"Where's her father's shop?" Dominic tried to sound casual as he avoided eye contact with the man, picking at a fingernail as he held his breath. The thought of not seeing Carianna again made his heart flutter with desperation.

Laughter rose above the crashing of the waves against the ferry. "Don't waste your time, kid. Carianna doesn't see things the way the rest of us do. She's special."

Dominic stayed quiet. *Yes, she is.* He didn't believe in spells either. But he was sure he'd fallen under one.

Chapter Two

Carianna pulled the screen door that led into her father's workroom, a crowded area in the back of the store that smelled like salt, fish, and stale cigarettes. She knew better than to tell her father about the man she'd met at San Jose Island. It would only upset him, and Carianna couldn't stand to see him unhappy.

She set the bag of shells on the workbench next to several sundials and a near perfect Shark Eye Carianna had brought him last week.

"Hello, Father," she said when the older man came into the workroom carrying a handful of silver chains, which he placed beside the shells.

Elijah Sparks coughed several times before he loosened the string on the knapsack and peered into the bag. Nodding, he lifted a starfish to eye level and smiled. "This is a nice one, Poppy." He stroked his gray beard as he fished out more shells. Carianna was used to her father calling her Poppy. Only when he was upset with her did he use her full name: Carianna Marie Sparks.

He put the starfish off to one side, then lined out the silver chains, sorting them by lengths. When he was done with that, her father filled his cleaning bowl with bleach and water. One-third bleach, two-thirds water. He dug several shells out of the bag and eased them into the metal container. Then he looked up at her and smiled, a movement that caused the wrinkles beneath his eyes to meet with the ones above his mouth. But it wasn't his happy smile, and Carianna knew right away that something was wrong.

"What is it, Father?" Carianna's heart beat faster as her hands started to sweat. "Tell me."

Hunched over and walking with a limp, her father shuffled to the bench nearby, the one he'd made when Carianna was a little girl. He'd taken a log that had washed up on the beach and carved it into a bench. There were pretty colored lines that ran the length of it, browns and oranges, and there was enough room for two people to sit down. Carianna recalled all the times her father had sat on that bench and read *A Captain's Tale* to her. She could still recite the story by heart, about a sailor who fought to be the captain of a big boat. Carianna saw it as her father's story, a tale he'd lived, with the only reminder of his journey being a dancing lady tattoo on his right arm. The man in the book never did get to be a captain, and neither did Elijah Sparks. Instead he got to be a father. *My father*.

Grimacing, the old man Carianna loved sat down on the bench and patted the seat beside him. They could see the ocean out the small window behind them, but Carianna studied her father's expression as his bushy eyebrows frowned inward. "What is it?" she asked him again.

"I am sick, Poppy." Her father reached for her hand and squeezed it in his. Carianna didn't move. Or breathe. Or squeeze his hand back. "And the good Lord is going to call me home sooner, rather than later."

Carianna's bottom lip trembled. Hurt and anger swirled into a tornado, stirring up her insides like someone turned on a blender inside her. "No. I don't think so. God would have told me."

She thought about the man on the beach. Dominic. His mother had died, and Carianna had told him that she was happy and with God. Wouldn't her father feel that same happiness Carianna had spoken of? She closed her eyes and began to silently count by eight as she squeezed her father's hand.

He eased away from her and twisted on the bench to face her. "Open your eyes and stop counting, Poppy. I need you to pay attention to what I'm saying."

Slowly she lifted her eyelids, which had suddenly become heavy. She stared at her father, willing him to take it back. He couldn't be sick. And God surely could not take him from her yet. Carianna had things to learn, things to do, places to go. "You promised me we would see other far away oceans. You promised that you would never leave me."

Her father shook his head. "No, Poppy. I did not promise that I would never leave you. We all leave. I promised you that I would not forsake you when you were young, a child who needed to be cared for. I promised you that I would not leave you to search for a way of life that felt better suited to me, the way your mother felt called to do. I promised that I would raise you proper." He paused as he pushed back strands of Carianna's hair from her face, the hint of a smile on his lips. "And I have." He sighed, and Carianna heard the familiar rattle in his chest as he breathed. "But I never said that I wouldn't leave you one day when my work was done. And I believe that day is coming."

They sat quietly for a while, and Carianna could hear and feel God knocking on her heart door, but she wasn't answering. She knew it was God. He was using the code word to get into her thoughts. God used a code word because He said there were others who would try to get into Carianna's heart, those who wouldn't have her best interests on their minds. "What kind of sick are you?" she finally asked.

Father made a fist and tapped lightly against his chest. "These ol' lungs are finally giving out, and the doctor said they are full of cancer."

"A disease caused by the uncontrolled division of abnormal cells in a part of the body." Carianna just knew certain things. Somehow she knew about cancer, but she had no idea how to tie her tennis shoes in double knots. She'd tried a thousand times.

"Yes, Poppy. That's what is making me sick. Nasty old cancer cells." He tried to smile again. "But you are going to be fine. You have Nanny and lots of friends who will keep a watchful eye on you."

Carianna frowned. "Nanny is ninety-four. I think I should be the one keeping a watchful eye on her." Millie Pence wasn't Carianna's grandmother, but she'd called the woman Nanny for as long as she could remember. Before she'd gotten really old, Nanny had run a café in a far away city, or so she'd said. Carianna wondered about it sometimes since Nanny didn't cook. But now the older woman mostly sat on the front porch shelling peanuts and eating them with the few teeth she had left. Peter was in her lap most of the time. Peter Cottontail, Nanny called him, because he had a white tail like the fabled bunny. Even though he was a black cat.

Her father touched her face as he blinked his eyes. "I have done the best that I can to prepare you for the challenges this life will bring you, Poppy." He eased his hand from her face and waved it around his work shed. "You know how to operate the tools necessary to keep our business going, from the Dremel drill to the sander. You've made necklaces, earrings, and beautiful knickknacks from the shells you've lovingly collected. This trade will provide you with a comfortable living."

Carianna shook her head. "You are wrong. It is not your time to go. Not yet. God would have told me, even if it was a whisper in my dreams."

"Do you remember all the things I began telling you when you started to become a woman?" Her father's cheeks flushed when he spoke of such things. "There will be those who will try to take advantage of your pure heart. Accept love, but be wary, the way I have been wary for you. While you must be cautious about outsiders not known to you, you must also be open to love."

"What kind of love?" Carianna sat taller as she crossed one leg over the other, recalling her conversation with God.

Her father hung his head. "The kind of love that a man and a woman share. The kind of love that exists especially for you, but such a man has not crossed over our threshold. And soon I won't be here to screen your suitors, Poppy."

Carianna felt like she should be crying, but she was convinced that he was not telling her the truth. Elijah didn't lie intentionally, but his words weren't true right now. She felt God knocking on the tiny door that led inside her heart. She gently opened for Him, but only enough to hear him whisper, "It is true, My child. Your earthly father will be leaving you soon." She slammed the door, stood up, and ran. All the way to the beach. At the water's edge, she bent at the waist, allowing the cool water to lap at her ankles as she wiggled her toes in the sand, tears burning her wind-burnt cheeks. Then she heard a voice. His voice. The man named Dominic.

"Are you okay?" Dominic leaned down, and even though he couldn't see her face, he knew it was her. *Carianna Marie Sparks.* God was blessing him abundantly today. First he'd had he best fish taco he'd ever had in his life for dinner. Then he'd gotten permission from his editor to stay as long as he needed. And now, here she was, the woman who'd occupied his thoughts since he'd laid eyes on her earlier in the day. A woman he'd met randomly, a person who had sent his heart fluttering, with only the wind dividing their kindred spirits. It was craziness. But here he was again, in her presence, having the same feelings.

She stood up, swiped at teary eyes, and upon recognizing Dominic, she took two bold steps backward, crossing her arms across her stomach. Dominic raised his palm to her.

"Wait. Don't run." He held his breath, fearful he'd chase her if she darted away, and he was sure that would scare her away for good. Easing off his windbreaker, he offered it to her. "Here, you're cold." He glanced around the beach, a high traffic area of Mustang Island. Condominiums side by side behind them. Nothing like the San Jose Island where they'd met this morning, a twenty-one mile stretch of beach that didn't have so much as a bathroom.

She took another step backward, her eyes wild with trepidation, widening with each second. Something primal in Dominic compelled him to push on, a protective instinct he didn't know he possessed. He was certain he'd give his life willingly for this woman he didn't know. Yet he was sure he'd known her forever, somehow. "Has someone hurt you?"

She nodded. "Yes."

Dominic balled his hands into fists at his sides, trembling. Partly from the chill in the air and surf's drizzle, but it was also an animal instinct to keep this woman safe. "Who? Where are they?" He peered up and down the beach, expecting an angry boyfriend to come into sight, despite what the guy on the boat had said, that Carianna's father wouldn't allow such a person in his daughter's life. "Who?" he asked again. "Who hurt you?"

Carianna lowered her hands to her sides as she took a took a step closer to him, pulling Dominic's blue windbreaker snug as loose strands of her hair danced with the wind. "You're Dominic Wayne Bennett."

Dominic smiled, the cool breeze suddenly warm and comforting, despite his bare arms. "And you're Carianna Marie Sparks." But as another tear spilled down her cheek, Dominic's muscles tensed. "Who hurt you Carianna?"

She stepped even closer, near enough to feel her breath against his face, near enough to see his image in her eyes. And for the second time in so many days, he wondered if this familiar stranger was going to kiss him. "Who hurt you?" he said in a whisper.

She leaned closer. "God."

Dominic raised an eyebrow. "As in, God the Father?" He pointed upward with one finger, wondering if he'd misheard her.

"The One and only." She crossed her arms across her chest, scowling in a way that seemed almost painful to her. "I am very upset with Him, and I will let Him know when we have tea on Thursday"

Have tea? Dominic opened his mouth to reply, but…he had no words just yet.

Chapter Three

Carianna wasn't sure how much to tell Dominic. How would she ever know whom to trust? She'd relied on her father not to leave her. And she had trusted God. *Forsaken by both.*

"My father is sick. He's going to die." She swallowed hard before a burning sensation lit up the side of her face, like when she ate ice cream too fast. "He just told me, and I—I'm …" Her voice sounded like a frog, croaky as she spat out the words.

"Oh, no." Dominic reached out to touch her arm. She let him, tempted to run, but his eyes met with hers, and a strange feeling swept over her like a blanket of warmth, yet she shivered. "I'm sure that was hard to hear."

He slowly lowered his arm, but she would have let him keep it there. "It *was* hard to hear. I can't imagine my life without my father." Carianna tried to envision what dying would be like. She pulled Dominic's jacket snug around her, then brushed hair from her face. "I wonder if dying is like being born. The bright light and swoosh of air filled my lungs until I thought I might explode. I felt my cheek against the warmth of my mother's chest. My mother's smile mixed with tears. And my father was there, his strong hand touching my back. God was there, of course." She fisted her hands and brought them to her chest. "There was so much love."

Dominic opened his mouth like he might say something, but then squinted at Carianna, even though the sun was behind them. He stared at her for a long time. "Do you want to walk down the beach?"

He must not remember being born. Carianna lowered her hands to her side, unable to keep her gaze from his lips. She wanted to trace the outline of his mouth with her finger, but that would seem odd. "Okay." She got in step with him.

"Does your father live with your mother?"

Carianna nudged Dominic away from a jellyfish that he was about to step on, then slowed her stride to study the tentacles. *Dead.* Sometimes, if they'd recently washed ashore, Carianna was able to use her shoe to help them back into the surf, and away they would go. *But not this one.*

"My mother left not long after I was born," she said as they started walking again.

"Your parents got divorced?"

Carianna slowed down, touched his arm, and coaxed him to stop, and she turned to face him. "No. They were never married. But Father said they had a great love." She studied Dominic, wondering if he would be her great love. His light brown hair was wavy, tousling in the breeze, and longer than most of the men she knew. Long enough to tuck a strand behind his ear. She reached up and did so. As she eased closer, she could see herself in his black sunglasses. Gently, she eased them off so she could see his eyes, which were as blue as the deepest part of the ocean. She edged closer to him, then brushed a finger against his lips as she drew her mouth to his.

Dominic trembled beneath her touch, his stomach in a wild swirl as her lips lightly touched his, like a whisper, the smell of her...the feel of her...intoxicating. He couldn't move. *Something is happening.* It wasn't physical. At twenty-nine, Dominic had kissed plenty of women, but if he hadn't known that to be a fact, he would have sworn this was his very first kiss. Feeling an intimacy of the soul so profound, he worried he might shed a tear. *This is crazy.*

He slowly released the breath he'd been holding when Carianna leaned away from him. "That was my first kiss." A gentle smile lit her face, slowly, as if she was discerning something about Dominic, reaching her hand into his soul. *What would she find?*

"What? That couldn't have been your first kiss," he said in a whisper as his heart thumped against his chest.

Carianna leaned closer to him, and Dominic smoothed her hair back, but at the last micro-second before her lips met his for a second time, he took his hands from her face, stared into her eyes, then gently latched onto her shoulders and eased her away. Based on something she'd said earlier, Carianna was in her mid twenties. "That couldn't have been your first kiss," he said again once some distance was between them.

"It was."

Dominic scratched his cheek, his eyes locked with hers.

"I think I'd like to do it again." She moved closer, but Dominic gently held her shoulders, keeping her a good foot away. Her expression fell.

"Carianna, there is nothing I want more in the world than to kiss you again," he said, understating his true desire for her. "But you don't even know me."

Dominic wasn't in the habit of taking advantage of women, and this was a clear case of such a thing if he let it go on. Carianna had never been kissed. She'd also said that she would be having tea with God, and she thought she remembered being born. *Walk away.*

Carianna might come across to someone else as being seductive, but she was most likely just enjoying the utopia of a first kiss. Dominic shivered as he considered what might have happened with another man, what he'd almost allowed to continue for himself.

"I know you," she finally said in barely a whisper. "God said you were coming." She smiled. "And here you are."

Dominic was rarely speechless. He was a reporter. But this beautiful creature had tied his tongue into so many knots he didn't know where to begin.

"I think I should walk you home," he finally said before he ran a hand through his windblown hair.

"Okay." She put her hand in his, and with shaky knees, Dominic started down the beach with her at his side, swinging hands like they'd been together forever.

This time, it was Dominic who felt the need to bolt, to run as fast and far away as he could from this woman. But, for the love of God, he couldn't. Maybe it was like the old man on the ferry had said, that Dominic was under her spell. Dominic didn't believe in spells. But as he and Carianna strolled down the beach hand in hand, he wondered how he could ever walk away from her.

At least, for now, she wasn't upset about her father. She'd seemed to toss that thought as soon as she'd had it, replacing it with focus on Dominic.

He was going to get her home safely, then soak up some rays back at the pool at his condo, and enjoy this plush gig he'd snagged. And never see her again.

They passed the high traffic area and grand entrance of Dominic's digs, then kept going until the high-rise condominiums grew smaller behind them. After a long stretch of mostly beach, with a few vacation houses here and there, Carianna tugged him toward a boardwalk staircase that took them over the sand dunes. On the other side, they walked through a condo parking lot and slipped into an ally that ran between two small real estate offices. When they emerged onto a side street, it was like stepping into another world, a line of shops in the distance that looked like they could have been there since the dawn of time.

As they got closer, Dominic saw a T-shirt store advertising 'two-for-ten dollars' etched into the window, and colorful garments hung on a rack outside blowing in the breeze. Next there was a small hut with a large handwritten sign that read *Tamales, Best on Mustang Island.*

To his right, there wasn't much, just vacant land with a For Sale sign and a few street vendors in portable structures selling jewelry, shells, dolphin statues, and other trinkets.

Everyone they passed waved at Carianna, and she responded to each person by name. Dominic didn't miss the fact that these people scowled at him. One woman even hissed. She was sitting on the porch shelling peanuts, and Dominic's stomach roiled when Carianna tugged him in that direction.

"Nanny, this is Dominic Wayne Bennett. He's twenty-nine," Carianna said, smiling, before she dropped Dominic's hand to lean down and kiss the old woman, who looked like she'd lived a whole lot of lives. Deep lines connected across proof that the lady had spent the entirety of her existence in the sun. She was wearing a loose brown dress that hit her below the knees, a huge contrast to the neon green Skechers running shoes she was wearing. Her gray hair was wound into a tiny bun on the top of her head, and dolphin earrings hung from each earlobe.

"Nice to meet you." Dominic extended his hand, and the woman latched on with a frail hand, but she squeezed hard enough to make him flinch.

"Nanny is ninety-four." Carianna smiled. She seemed to be mildly obsessed with numbers, or ages.

"I was just walking Carianna home, but I should probably go now." Dominic forced the best smile he could come up with as he glanced at the bamboo sign overhead. *The Shell Collector.*

Carianna's eyes followed his and lifted. "Father has been called the shell collector since he was a boy. He grew up here on Mustang Island. He knows more about shells than anyone in the world, and his creations are original and sought after."

Dominic nodded, then he smiled at Nanny, wondering what her real name was. She didn't smile back. Instead, she drew her eyebrows in, to a point that Dominic thought she might be causing herself pain, her mouth puckering into a downward slant.

"I, uh, should be going. Nice to meet you, Nanny." Dominic gave a wave of his hand toward the old woman before he turned to Carianna. "I enjoyed our, um...walk."

Carianna rushed to him, stopping so close that he felt her breathe. "Wait here while I get my father."

Dominic was about to argue, but then Carianna smiled, and wild horses couldn't have carried him away. *Yep, she's got me under a spell.* A spell he needed to break.

Carianna dashed off, and Dominic turned his attention to the old Nanny, just as she cracked a peanut and stuffed it in between her thin lips, dropping the shell in a pile between her shoes. He thought about making a run for it before Carianna came back and drew him to her like a magnet to steel. But his feet rooted to the dirt beneath them. This inlet reminded him of something he'd seen in an old western movie—a saloon on one side, lines of wooden shops, horses and buggies going up and down the middle of the street. *Western with a beach flair.*

"Have you always lived on the island?" Dominic swiped at a bee that landed on his forehead, causing his sunglasses to fall off. He leaned down to pick them up, and when he straightened, the old woman was smiling. She had two visible teeth in her mouth. Both right in the front, which made her look like a very old rabbit. But she didn't answer.

Dominic glanced at the glass window of the shop, filled with shell necklaces, wind chimes, picture frames, and he took note of a small Capiz shell chandelier that his mother would have loved. "Maybe I'll just go on in." Dominic pointed to the door to the right of the window, where Carianna had gone.

Nanny picked up another peanut and pressed it between her fingers, keeping her eyes down.

It didn't stop her from stretching out one of her green Skechers just as Dominic walked past her. Thankfully, he stopped in time. He was more concerned that he could have broken the woman's leg, as opposed to her tripping him, as she'd surely intended.

Carianna pulled the door open about the same time Nanny withdrew her foot back to the pile of peanut shells.

"I wasn't sure if Father was in the workroom or if he was inside the store, but he's in here. Come in to meet him." Carianna locked eyes with Dominic in a way that left him feeling almost woozy, and on shaky legs, he moved toward her. He stopped right before the entrance when he saw a penny on the ground. He picked it up and saw that it was a wheat penny. "My mom always said these were lucky." He smiled, and Carianna led him in.

Dominic looked over his shoulder at the old woman right before he crossed the threshold.

She cinched her face, as if trying to make it smaller, and crinkled her nose as she stuck her tongue out at him.

Dominic hurried inside the shop, not having high hopes about how well he would be received by the shell collector. He took a deep breath.

Chapter Four

"This is Dominic Wayne Bennett," Carianna said to her father. Since she'd bumped into Dominic twice, and considering what God had told her, she thought Dominic and her father should be introduced. "We met on San Jose Island, but we saw each other again here, on Mustang Island." She looked at Dominic for what she intended to be only a few seconds, but her gaze stayed on him. Forcing her eyes away, she turned to her father, who scowled. "His mother died recently." The comment caused her thoughts to shift to her father's health, but her father's serious expression softened at that news.

"I am sorry for your loss, Dominic." Father wiped his hand on his black apron, then extended it to Dominic. "I'm Elijah."

"Thank you, sir. It was a few months ago, but …"

Carianna put a hand to her chest and felt her heart pumping wildly. She wanted to hug Dominic, and she wanted to kiss him again, kiss away his pain. But she was sure that would be inappropriate right now. "Father, I'd like to invite Dominic to have supper with us."

Dominic cleared his throat. "Uh, no. That's okay. You don't have to do that. And, I've got work to do when I get back to my condo."

"But you have to eat. Father says he works better on a full stomach." She paused to study her father's face and waited for him to agree with her, but he only rubbed his chin, staring at Dominic. *Oh, dear.* Her eyes darted back to Dominic, pleading with him to stay. These feelings were confusing, but she was sure she didn't want him to leave.

Her father looked at Dominic. "You should stay. Carianna is making crab cakes, and I promise you, they are the best crab cakes you will ever have."

Carianna smiled at her father and thanked him with her eyes.

∽

Dominic recalled what the old man on the ferry had told him. *Carianna's father is a force to be reckoned with if he thinks anyone is interested in his daughter.* He had been sure Elijah would have discouraged Dominic from staying for a meal. Since he hadn't, Dominic wasn't sure how to proceed. But his mouth watered at the thought of crab cakes.

Carianna's smile and hopeful eyes were on Dominic as he said, "I guess I would work better on a full stomach." And despite his concerns about leading Carianna on in his attempt to do the right thing, the thought of leaving her twisted him into knots.

"You visit with Father." Carianna lifted on her toes as she pressed her palms together. "I'm going to prepare the meal."

Dominic's eyes followed her until she had exited via a back door in the shop. When he turned back to Elijah, the older man ran a hand the length of his beard, his eyes fixated on Dominic, brows narrowing into a frown. Dominic braced himself, but when the man didn't say anything, Dominic glanced around the small shop and eyed some of Elijah's creations. He picked up a shined conch horn, admired it, and then turned his attention to a pair of shells next to the conch. "Lightening whelks, state shell of Texas," he said softly as he eyed the other shells on the shelf closest to him.

"You know shells?" Elijah limped toward him, a bit hunched over. Dominic assumed Carianna's parents must have had her late in life. Elijah looked more like Carianna's grandfather.

Dominic shrugged. "A little. I wrote a paper in college about shells and the values attached to some of them. Unbelievable the prices people get for some of the rare ones."

Elijah motioned with his hand for Dominic to follow him, and they made a slow trek to a cased enclosed in glass in the corner. Elijah pulled a key from his pocket and unlocked it. He pointed to one of the shells as he lifted an eyebrow. "Familiar with this?"

Dominic leaned closer. "Scaphella junonia?"

Elijah nodded as he picked up the shell. "Yes. Carianna found this treasure. It will fetch over a hundred dollars." He handed it to Dominic. "Actually, Carianna has brought home most of what's in here. She's been riding the ferry to San Jose Island every Friday for about twelve years. I don't think she's ever missed a Friday."

"It's a beauty." Dominic carefully handed the shell back to him and waited while he locked it back up, alongside some other more valuable items. Then Elijah bent over slightly and covered his mouth with his hand as he coughed.

"When I ran into Carianna on the beach, she was upset about your health. I'm sorry to hear about that." Dominic cleared his throat, hoping he wasn't overstepping.

Elijah stroked his beard again, his eyes locked with Dominic's. "Carianna feels things in a way that other people do not. My passing will be difficult for her."

"You sound as if there isn't any hope. What about chemo or other treatments?" Dominic stuffed his hands in the pockets of his Khaki shorts.

Elijah raised a shoulder and dropped it slowly, rather nonchalantly. "There isn't any hope. I'm going to die. Carianna must prepare herself for that. Good Lord willing, Nanny will still be here to comfort her when that time comes."

Dominic couldn't imagine Nanny being a comfort to anyone, but he nodded, thinking that Elijah wasn't the force to be reckoned with that he'd expected. "What is Nanny's real name?"

"Millie. She isn't Carianna's grandmother any more than she's my mother." Elijah covered his mouth before he coughed again, this time pulling a handkerchief out of his pants pocket, raising it to his mouth. "But Carianna found her walking aimlessly on the beach one winter, barefoot, cold, and hungry. She brought her home, nursed her to good health, and the old gal just never left. She's lived in a room we built onto the back of our house for about fifteen years, give or take."

"Is your house attached to the shop?" Dominic wondered if the door Carianna used to leave the shop went directly to their home.

"More or less. A hop, skip, and a jump." Elijah coughed into the cloth again.

"Lung cancer?" Dominic could smell the stench of cigarette smoke when the man had walked close to him, and there was a faint, but lingering aroma in the shop.

Elijah nodded, still hacking into the handkerchief. Dominic was about to ask Elijah if he needed something to drink when the back door swung wide. Carianna rushed to her father with a large glass.

"I can hear you coughing from in the kitchen." She pushed the glass in his direction. "Here. It's raspberry tea."

Elijah wiped his mouth before taking a gulp of the tea. *Raspberry tea.* Dominic loved raspberry tea, even though he thought of it as something a bunch of women would order at brunch. "Thank you, Poppy."

Dominic looked at Carianna.

"Father has called me Poppy for as long as I can remember. It's short for the Latin name *Poppaea.* When Father was in the Army, he met a beautiful woman named Poppaea. He said she was a princess and the most beautiful woman he'd ever met. Until I was born." She smiled before she said something in another language. *"Maxime pulchra mulier."*

Dominic scratched his chin. *That sounded like Latin.* "What does that mean?"

"It's Latin for 'the most beautiful woman'." She lowered her gaze, blushing a little.

Maybe she only knew a phrase or two, but he had to ask. "Do you know Latin?"

"Of course. The crab cakes are in the oven." Carianna touched Dominic's arm. "I'm glad you stayed."

"Me too." It was true, despite his strong reservations. But nothing was going to get out of hand with Carianna's father around. Dominic just needed to avoid being alone with her.

"See you in a while then." She spun on her heel and left Dominic with Elijah, who took another long drink of tea.

"How did she learn Latin?"

Maybe it was the way Dominic said it that caused Elijah to grin. "How did she learn Latin?" He shrugged, motioning for Elijah to follow him. "How, also, did she learn French, Spanish, and German?" The old man looked over his shoulder as he walked, then chuckled. "Come on Dominic Wayne Bennett. I'll give you the two-cent tour of our humble abode."

Dominic forced his gaping mouth closed, and he slowly followed Elijah, wondering what else he would learn about Carianna.

They walked out the door and into a small courtyard. Then Elijah opened another door that led into a modest living room with a blue and white couch, a tan recliner, and an enormous bookshelf along one wall. A wonderful aroma filled the space, and as Dominic breathed in the succulent smells of garlic, onion cooking, and something wonderful he couldn't identify, his eyes landed on the books.

"Carianna likes to read," Elijah said when he saw Dominic ogling the titles. He gingerly ran a hand along the binding of *Moby Dick*, along with *Catcher In the Rye* and *Little Women*.

"I read a lot too." Dominic continued his scan of the classics along the third shelf from the top.

Elijah sat down in the recliner, pulled a knob on the side, and kicked his feet out, motioning for Dominic to take a seat on the couch. There was a TV tray on either side of the couch, and a small coffee table in front of him with a box of tissues and a *People* magazine with an actress Dominic didn't recognize on the cover.

"Carianna buys those." Elijah pointed to the magazine. "She prays for the people inside who are having problems, those going through a divorce or some other horrific event."

Dominic nodded, touched, if not taken aback a little.

"What do you do for work, Dominic?" Elijah adjusted his weight in the chair, grimacing as he settled into the worn recliner.

"I'm a reporter. I'm actually here because I'm doing a piece on the ten best islands for shell collecting, and San Jose Island is one of them."

"I see." Elijah studied him. "So you will be leaving soon?"

Dominic took a deep breath and sighed. "Yeah, I will be. In a few days."

"I see," he repeated, his voice clipped now. "Carianna gets close to people very easily. She trusts everyone, and she finds the good in every person she meets, even if it's buried far beneath the surface." He paused. "I don't know you, and I have no way to know how much good you've got in you, but I suspect Poppy will find it and latch onto it. But I will trust you not to allow yourself to get close to her." His eyes blazed as he paused. "And I mean that in every sense of the word."

Ah, here is the force to be reckoned with. "I hear you, sir, and I will respect your wishes. We just met, so …" Dominic shrugged, but pulled his eyes away from Carianna's father as he recalled the kiss on the beach. He took a deep breath, breathing in the heavenly aroma wafting into the room from the kitchen. "It sure smells good. I'm looking forward to the crab cakes. Thank you for having me in your home."

Elijah nodded as he picked up a pair of gold-rimmed reading glasses on the table, then a newspaper nearby.

Dominic assumed the conversation was over, and when the silence became awkward, he got up and strolled along the bookcase, taking an occasional glance around the room. Then he realized something was missing. There wasn't a TV. He took another look, but no television. *Could they not afford one?* If that was the case, where did they get all of these books? Everyone had a TV. He cleared his throat.

"I noticed you don't have a television, or maybe it's in another room?"

"There are no TVs in our house."

Dominic moved his mouth from one side to the other, considering the reasons why not.

Elijah took off his reading glasses and looked up at Dominic, still standing by the bookcase. Sighing, he said, "It upsets Carianna, especially the news." He lifted the newspaper. "I read everything I need to know, and the only thing I've missed about television is football, but that upsets Poppy too."

"Football upsets her?" Dominic tucked his hands in the back of his pockets as he turned to face the man. "Why?"

Elijah smiled slightly. "She doesn't agree with a bunch of grown men pushing each other down for sport."

Dominic grinned, nodding. He wasn't into spectator sports, although he loved to participate. Tennis, softball, and basketball when he was able to get his buddies together, which was less and less these days.

His stomach rumbled as he picked up a copy of *Wuthering Heights* then returned to the couch with it. Flipping through the pages, he looked up when the front door opened.

Nanny—Millie—stepped across the threshold leaning on a cane, still wearing her neon green Skechers and brown sack dress. She shuffled toward the couch, and Dominic held his breath as the old woman sat down beside him.

"Hello, Dominic. So nice to see you again." She pressed her mouth into a thin smile, not revealing her bunny teeth, and her voice was thick and sweet as syrup. The woman could have been anyone's darling, precious grandmother, not an old lady who had tried to trip Dominic and stuck her tongue out at him. *I'll play along.* He released the breath he was holding.

"Nice to see you again also." He forced a smile, noticing the woman kept her hand on her cane. Dominic wondered briefly if she might bop him over the head with it.

"Will you be joining us for supper?" Millie batted her eyes at him. "I do believe I smell Carianna's crab cakes in the oven."

Dominic glanced at Elijah, who had his head buried in the newspaper. Then he turned back to Millie. "Yes, I've been invited to stay for dinner."

Millie stared long and hard at Dominic, but he returned to flipping the pages of the book, keeping one eye on Granny Dearest.

Chapter Five

Carianna lit two candles in the middle of the kitchen table, and she'd already set out plates, napkins, and silverware. The crab cakes were keeping warm in the oven, so she pulled the salad she'd made from the refrigerator. Every time she thought about Dominic, her heart thumped wildly against her chest. He was basically a stranger, but as she reached up and touched her lips, she recalled their kiss, and he didn't feel like a stranger. Somehow, she was sure this was the man God had told her about. That knowledge elated and terrified her all at the same time. But why hadn't God informed her about her father's health? Carianna thought that she and God had an open, honest relationship, and it still angered her that He hadn't prepared her for this.

She tapped a finger to her chin as she glanced around the small kitchen, wondering what she'd forgotten. *Tea and glasses.*

Pulling the pitcher of raspberry tea from the refrigerator, she set it on the table, then took four glasses from the cabinet and placed them on the table as well. She took a final look before she walked into the living room to tell everyone dinner was ready. Dominic was the first one to stand up and head her way.

"Dominic you can sit there," she said, pointing to the chair across from her father. It was a small space in the corner of the room where the table and chairs barely fit. "It's snug." She smiled at Dominic as her stomach swirled and flipped. Wondering if he would like the meal, she pondered about what type of home Dominic lived in. Was it modest and simple like hers? Or was it fancy?

"Wow." Dominic sat down. "This looks amazing."

Once everyone was seated, her father and Nanny bowed their heads, and then Dominic did as well.

Carianna cleared her throat. "I would prefer if someone else asks the blessing."

All three people opened their eyes and lifted their heads, but it was her father who turned to her and said, "Poppy, you always ask the blessing."

Carianna's chest tightened. "Not tonight." She glanced at Dominic, then at her father and Nanny.

"Perhaps our guest would like to lead us in prayer?" Nanny smiled at Dominic, who nodded.

"Happy to." They all bowed their heads. "Dear Lord, we thank you for this food and the many blessings you bestow on us each and every day. And we thank you for new friendships. Amen."

Carianna smiled. She loved listening to someone pray aloud in front of her for the first time. There was an intimacy about it, like listening in on a private conversation She repeated the prayer to herself eight times, hoping to find a way to forgive God for choosing not to heal her father. She wasn't sure that was possible.

Dominic finished the best crab cakes he'd ever had, and when Carianna asked him if he wanted to go for a walk on the beach, he thought of several reasons he could give to decline her request. Instead, he breezily said, "Sure."

Elijah's eyes darted in Dominic's direction, but the older man didn't say anything. Millie offered to clean the kitchen when Carianna began to clear the table.

"Are you sure, since we usually do it together?" Carianna hooked her thumbs in the back pockets of her blue jeans.

Millie nodded, winked at Carianna, and said, "You kids just have a good time."

Once again, the woman's voice was sweet as southern iced tea.

Elijah slowly lifted himself up and limped toward the living room, coughing almost the entire time. Dominic wondered how much time Elijah had.

"I just need to get my sweater." Carianna smiled. "Be right back."

Dominic kept his head down, but he could feel Millie's eyes on him so he slowly looked up at her and forced a smile.

Millie held her hands up as if they were paws scratching in his direction. Then she actually hissed at him. By now, Dominic figured he shouldn't be stunned by her antics, but he found himself speechless just the same. Carianna was back before Dominic could formulate a sentence that didn't go along with what he was thinking, which was, *you are nuts lady*.

Carianna latched onto Dominic's hand, gave a quick wave to Millie, then she paraded Dominic across the living room in front of her father, still hand in hand.

Elijah narrowed his eyebrows, his eyes honed in on Carianna and Dominic's hands. But they were out the door before Elijah had time to comment.

"The moon is two days away from being completely full," Carianna said once they were on the beach. She was still holding his hand, and Dominic was glad since there were two guys approaching them from the opposite direction. Both had on black hoodies, and one of them was carrying what appeared to be a metal detector. Something didn't feel right. Dominic held tighter to Carianna's hand and slowed their stride.

As the light of the moon reflected off the ocean, illuminating the space around them, Dominic looked past the men, but there was not a soul in sight. He swallowed hard and turned sharply to his left, pulling Carianna along with him. He headed in the direction of one of the condominiums where plenty of outdoor lights flooded the surrounding grounds.

"Something is wrong," Carianna whispered.

"I know. I can feel it too." Dominic kept his eyes ahead of them, picking up the pace, but Carianna slowed down, let go of his hand, and faced him.

"What do you feel?" she asked as she brought a hand to her chest. "The sadness?"

Dominic reached for her hand again, but missed in the darkness. "Come on. We need to go." He looked toward the two men. They were at the water's edge, but looking at Dominic.

"No. We can't go. They need our help." Carianna jogged away from Dominic as his palms grew sweaty.

"Carianna, wait!" He jogged after her and caught up to her just after she'd stopped in front of the two guys.

"Hey," Dominic said to the men, both of whom towered over Dominic. He could see they were older than he'd thought, maybe mid-thirties. "Carianna, we need to go." Dominic found her hand, but missed latching onto it.

"What have you lost?" Carianna pulled her black sweater snug around her. Dominic held his breath, wondering when he'd become so paranoid, but there was no missing the knife strapped to one guy's belt. And when the man unsnapped the sheath, Dominic's heart hammered against his chest. He couldn't take them both. One had a knife, and the other guy could swing that metal detector and knock him out with one blow.

"A piece of jewelry," the guy on the left said. He had a fair complexion and freckles covering most of his face, which might have lent him a youthful look if not for the lines of time that feathered at the corner of each eye. The other man pulled off his hoodie and revealed a thick dark mane that fell to his shoulders. Guy two had a gold tooth right in the front of his mouth.

Dominic knew better than to judge a person by looks, but he was struggling not to as his eyes drifted back to the knife.

Carianna stepped closer to the knife wielding man. "This is high tide. It will be very hard to find anything now. Low tide is at six tomorrow morning. If you'd like, we can meet back here at that time. I can help you look for whatever it is that you lost." She smiled. "How does that sound?"

Dominic glanced at Carianna, her face always aglow with hope, but what were the chances of finding a piece of lost jewelry? Worse than a needle in a haystack. But then he recalled the sunglasses he'd lost in Hawaii, on a trip with his parents when he was a kid. He'd lost the glasses in the surf, and for three days he looked for them every morning. He'd spent his allowance to buy them. At twelve, twenty-four dollars had seemed like a lot. On day four of his search, he'd stepped on them when he was thigh deep in the waves. *Maybe not such a stretch after all.*

He took a deep breath as the guy fumbled with the strap on the knife. Carianna didn't have a purse, but Dominic's wallet stuck out of his back pocket about a quarter inch.

Both guys looked at each other and grinned. Dominic tried to center all of his strength in his legs, so that he could push Carianna back and get in front of her if he needed to, and thrust a kick where it would count, if he needed to.

The knife guy pulled on the knife, shot a look at Dominic, then let his gaze drift back to Carianna. "Yeah, whatever, I guess."

"Wonderful. We will see you here tomorrow."

Dominic forced a smile, found Carianna's hand, and drug her to their left as he gave a quick wave to the men. *Dear God, don't let them follow us.* He looked over his shoulder twice, but the men had moved on, and Dominic's heart rate was slowly getting back to normal. He stopped her when they reached a courtyard entrance that went into the large building.

"Didn't you see that guy's knife?" He faced her and gently put his hands on her forearms. "He had unsnapped the scabbard. You can't be so trusting, Carianna."

She stared at him for a long while. "They weren't going to hurt us."

Dominic dropped his arms to his side and hung his head for a few seconds, wondering how Carianna had survived by being this naïve. He looked back at her. "You don't know that. It's best to avoid strangers, especially big guys like that when it's almost dark. Do you make a habit of approaching people like that?"

"If you believe people are bad, then you give them the power to be that way." She shrugged. "But if you treat people with goodness, it overflows to them."

Dominic stared at her, his jaw dropped slightly. "Carianna…" Dominic thought about what her father had said, how the news on TV upsets her. "You can't be that trusting with total strangers."

"Yes, I can." She walked away from him, heading back toward her house.

Dominic walked alongside her as his eyes scanned the beach. The two men were gone. Or so it appeared.

"Those guys were big. I'm almost six foot tall, but they were, uh, like six-four. Didn't you feel threatened at all, or a little nervous?" Dominic glanced over his shoulder, peering into total darkness now, wishing the moon were at its full peak.

She slowed down and faced him, holding his cheeks in her hands, which were warm from being in the pockets of her sweater. Then she lifted on her toes to kiss him gently on the lips. "Don't worry so much." She smiled.

Dominic wanted to pull her into his arms and kiss her until the sun came up, but Elijah's words hung in his mind. And he didn't want to take advantage of her. What if the kissing led to something else? If Dominic was Carianna's first kiss…he was sure there were a lot of other firsts she hadn't experienced. But one thing was for sure. He'd never felt such a fierce need to protect another person.

He'd been involved in several fights, mostly in his late teens and once when he was twenty-one, but it wasn't his nature to be physical. Yet he would have died trying to protect Carianna if it had come to that, and he barely knew her. Would he have done that for any woman, or was it something about her that drew out this primal protectiveness?

They were quiet most of the way back to her house. Dominic decided he'd see her home safely, then stay close to the row of condominiums on the way back to his own room. After that, he was going to walk away from Carianna Marie Sparks for good.

At the front door to her house, Dominic was relieved Millie wasn't in her rocking chair, but he could see movement inside the house, a shadow as someone moved through the living room.

"Is your Nanny okay in the head? When you're not around, she kind of treats me weird."

Carianna chuckled softly. "What?"

Dominic lifted a shoulder before he dropped it slowly and said, "She stuck her tongue out at me, hissed at me, and tried to trip me." He grinned. "Just wondering if that's how she treats everyone, or if it's just me."

Carianna's eyes rounded as she smiled. "That sounds silly. Why would she do those things?"

"I have no idea." He shook his head, still grinning, when Carianna kissed him on the cheek.

"See you tomorrow?" She raised an eyebrow.

"Uh …" *Walk away.* "Uh, I probably need to work on my article tomorrow, but thank you for that amazing dinner and for having me in your home."

"You are very welcome."

They stood staring at each other for a while before Dominic's stomach lurched a little. "You're not going to meet those guys on the beach tomorrow, are you?"

Her expression fell slightly. "Of course I am. I told them I would."

Dominic took a deep breath, fairly sure he couldn't talk her out of such an idea, but willing to give it a shot. "I seriously doubt they will find what they've lost. Instead, why don't I pick you up in my rental car, and we can go eat breakfast somewhere?"

She shook her head. "Father makes kolaches on Saturday."

Dominic's palate came to attention. He loved the Czech pastries common to Texas. A dollop of fruit surrounded by pillowing dough.

"And besides …" she said, "I promised those two men that I would help them."

Dominic sighed. Kolaches or not, he couldn't let her go alone. "Well, don't leave without me. I'll be here at a little before six, and we'll go together."

Carianna smiled at him, then walked inside.

So much for just walking away from her.

Chapter Six

Dominic lightly rapped on Carianna's front door the next morning, and when she opened it, she had a basket draped over her arm, the contents covered by a red and white checkered towel. "I thought I would bring the men some of Father's kolaches, along with some coffee." She smiled. "I have some for us also."

He nodded. "Thanks." Dominic wondered if crazy Millie or Carianna's father ever questioned her comings and goings. If Dominic weren't here, Carianna would be flitting off to the beach toting pastries and coffee for two guys who didn't appear to be the most upstanding citizens on Mustang Island.

It was exactly six o'clock when they reached the same spot on the beach.

"Where are they?" Carianna let the basket slide from her elbow to her wrist as she frowned. "Maybe they're just late."

Maybe they aren't coming. Dominic zipped his jacket as the sharp breeze blew through the windbreaker. "More kolaches for us," he said, hoping to lift her expression as her sun-kissed brown locks danced in the gusty air, sending them whipping across her face. The basket was in her hand now as she stared out at the sea, then turned and scanned both directions along the beach.

She pulled a dark blue blanket from the bottom of the basket; similar to the ones Dominic received during air travel. She put it on the ground, set the basket on top of it, then sat down.

Dominic lowered himself and folded his legs crisscross beneath himself. "It's a gorgeous sunrise, huh?" Orange hues met with shades of blue as the sun lifted above the horizon.

Carianna nodded, but her eyes drifted down the beach again, peering one way, then the other. Blinking her eyes a few times, she finally unwrapped the checkered towel and revealed eight fruit-filled pastries. "Four are apple kolaches, two are filled with strawberries and cream cheese, and these …" She pointed to the last two. "…are apricot."

Dominic's mouth watered as he eyed the offerings. "Which is your favorite?"

"I like them all, but if I had to choose, I'd pick apple."

Dominic reached for one of the strawberry and cream cheese kolaches. Carianna opened a thermos of coffee and poured them each a cup. Dominic savored the flavor of the fruit pastry, followed by a swig of coffee, as the sun cleared the horizon and brought forth a new day.

"You look beautiful," he whispered, unable to take his eyes off of her this morning. She wore a red, hooded jacket, much like the black hoodies the guys wore the night before. Dominic wondered if that was intentional. Hers had a picture of a guitar on it with *Nashville* printed underneath.

"I love Nashville," he said before he took a bite of the pastry. After he swallowed, he asked, "Have you been there?"

Carianna shook her head. "No. A friend of Father's gave me this as a gift. I hope to go there someday." She looked up and down the beach, and there was no mistaking the disappointment in her eyes.

"Nashville is a cool place. Next to Texas, it's my favorite place to eat." Dominic finished the kolache. "And, without a doubt, the Grand Ole' Opera is awesome."

Carianna whipped her head back to him. "Have you traveled a lot of places?"

Dominic nodded. "Yeah, mostly because of my job. But I'm tired of traveling so much. I'd like to lay down some roots soon. I live in my parents' house, the house I grew up in on the outskirts of Houston. Sometimes, I'm happy to be there since it's filled with so many memories. Other times, it makes me miss my parents even more." He shrugged. "It's too much room for me anyway. I'm thinking about selling it."

"I've never been out of Texas, and I've only traveled with Father a few times."

Dominic stopped chewing and stared at her. "What?" he asked with a mouthful. He finished off the kolache. "How can that be?"

She shrugged. "It's okay. Father and I made plans to travel to places farther away several times, but it never seemed to happen. Then Nanny came along, and we've been afraid to leave her alone for long. She forgets to take her medications if we don't remind her."

Dominic thought about the five-minute ferry ride from Mustang Island to Aransas Pass. Then he thought about the short ferry ride from Mustang Island to San Jose Island, where they'd met. Carianna had probably taken those ferries back and forth hundreds of times. "You've never been anywhere outside of Texas?"

She shook her head, still taking her gaze back and forth down the beach.

"If you could go anywhere in the world, where would you go?"

Her face lit up with a smile. "I have a travel book, and I've marked all the places I'd like to see. There's too many to list."

"What's the number one place on your bucket list?"

She tapped a finger to her chin. "The Grand Canyon."

Dominic smiled. "I've been a lot of places, but I've never seen the Grand Canyon."

Carianna stared at him for a few moments. "Where will you go when you leave here?"

His chest tightened at the thought of leaving, but he'd only known this woman for twenty-four hours. "I'm scheduled to go to Marco Island in Florida. It's on the Top 10 list of the best beaches for shell collecting. Coming here, and then taking the ferry to San Jose Island was my first stop."

"When are you leaving?"

Dominic held her eyes in his gaze as he tried to decipher her expression. Was she sad he was leaving? He couldn't tell. "I'm supposed to leave Tuesday."

"Then why do you think we met? I feel like I've known you for a long time." She tucked her hair behind her ears as she tipped her head to one side, staring at him.

"I—I don't know." Dominic suspected she felt that way because of the kiss. Elijah's comments marched to the front of his mind and squatted there like a soldier on duty. But Dominic had to question why he felt the same way. "It's almost like I dreamed about you, or something. You're just ..." He paused, his heart pounding in his chest. "You're beautiful. The most beautiful person I've ever seen. But it's something else. There's a familiarity about you." *And I feel the need to take care of you for the rest of my life.* Which was crazy indeed.

She smiled again. "I think you're beautiful too."

Dominic grinned a little as he felt his cheeks warm. Handsome would have been the word he hoped for, but he'd happily settle for beautiful, coming from her.

Carianna scooted closer to him, until their knees were touching and she was close enough to kiss. *Lord, help me, I won't be able to say no.* But she brought a hand to her chest. "You are beautiful on the inside, too, and not everyone is."

"How can you know that?" Dominic held his breath. He'd felt like she was seeing his soul since the first moment he'd laid eyes on her.

She shrugged, but stayed close. "I don't know, but it's true."

They were quiet for a while. Dominic had two days left with her, then an early flight on Tuesday. He was tempted to cancel his flight and stay with her forever.

"I have tea with God on Thursdays. I plan to talk to him about you, along with my thoughts about Father."

Dominic opened his mouth to say something, but was at a loss. Her statement was a firm reminder that after today, Dominic needed to carry on with his life, the same way Carianna would carry on with hers.

"It's going to be a hard conversation because I've never been this angry with Him before. I *need* my father, and I can't imagine my life without him. And he's going to die."

"Maybe not. Miracles happen." He waited, but when she didn't say anything, he decided to lead her in the same direction she'd taken him when he told her about his mother. "And, even if he does, he will be happy and healthy in heaven, right? That's what you told me about my mother. It still hurts when I think about her, and I guess it will for a long time, but I choose to believe that she's in heaven and dancing with the angels."

Carianna smiled. "There's nothing more beautiful than when the angels dance."

"You mean...you can envision them dancing in your mind, right?"

Dominic cringed a little when she shook her head.

"No. I've danced with them before. I can't dance the way they do, but it's heavenly to watch them and to try."

Walk away, the little voice in his head shouted. But the thought hadn't even cleared his mind when another, stronger voice said *stay*.

"Can I take you to dinner tomorrow night?"

She didn't answer, just stared at him. As she moved closer and her lips brushed with his, Dominic saw Elijah's face again, but the more Carianna kissed him, the more out of focus Elijah became, until the older man's image vanished from his mind's eye. He cupped her cheeks, pulling her closer, and again, it was an intimacy he couldn't put into words. Two souls become one. It sounded corny, even in his mind, but he had no other way to describe what he was feeling.

"Sure. I'd love to have dinner with you tomorrow night."

Carianna slowly put some distance between them, and her eyes went somewhere over Dominic's shoulder. "I wonder why those two men didn't show up."

He thought about her life after he was gone. "Carianna, I don't think you should talk to or hang out with those guys if you see them again."

"Why?"

"I'm just not sure they're good guys."

"But are you *sure* they're bad?"

Dominic raised a shoulder and let it fall slowly. "Well, no...but ..."

"If you go through life expecting evil, that's what you will find."

"It's not that easy." Dominic dropped his sunglasses down over his eyes when they started to burn a little. Not so much from the sun's glare, but more to disguise what he felt, fearful she'd see it in his eyes. He'd run across many types of evil in his life.

"I guess we'll see," she said in a breezy whisper as her eyes trailed past him.

Dominic turned around. The same two guys in the same two black hoodies were strolling up the beach toward them.

And it was early in the morning in the off-season. Not a soul on the beach.

If the guys were still looking for a piece of jewelry, where was the metal detector they had before?

Carianna stood up and started toward the men before Dominic could organize his thoughts and discourage her.

He got in step with her and said a quick prayer.

Chapter Seven

Dominic could smell the two guys, the aroma of beer and sweat coasting ahead of them in the breeze. The one man still had a knife holstered on his hip, and just like the night before, his hand was resting on it. Dominic pushed his sunglasses up on his head and took a deep breath. If they'd wanted to hurt them or rob them, they could have done so last night when it was dark. It seemed unlikely that they'd start any trouble in broad daylight, even if it were too early for most people to be walking the beach. Although in the distance, Dominic saw a lady walking a huge dog along the waterline.

"Hey, did you find what you were looking for?" Dominic forced a smile. He could smell the stench more strongly now. Lots of people smoke, drink, and sweat, he reminded himself. It didn't mean they were bad guys.

"Uh, yeah, man. We found it." The guy on the left slurred a little as he spoke, but it was the eerie grin on his friend's face that was the most unnerving.

"I'm so glad you found it." Carianna had picked up the kolaches, the four left that were wrapped in foil. "My father made these this morning. I brought some for you."

The guy on the left took his hand off the knife and accepted the gift.

"Oh, I brought coffee too." She held up a finger. "Be right back."

She hadn't been gone two seconds when the man on the right lifted the front of his black hoodie, just enough to show his belly hanging slightly over worn jeans. And the gun tucked into his pants.

"Just be cool," the guy said in a deep voice, his dark eyes hooded like a hawk, a half smile crooked up on one side.

Dominic's heart beat so fast, he was sure they could see it pounding beneath his windbreaker. "You can have whatever you want. Don't hurt her." He spoke firmly even though there was no way he could take on both of these hulks, even if they hadn't been packing a pistol and a knife.

"Here is some coffee for you." Carianna handed them each a cup. "I'm Carianna Marie Sparks, and this is Dominic Wayne Bennett."

"Uh, yeah." The man on the left turned to his buddy, and they both grinned. "I'm John, and that's James."

Dominic doubted that was their real names.

"John and James were the names of two of Jesus' disciples." Carianna smiled. "But I'm guessing you know that."

Dominic couldn't move. His legs shook. The roar of the ocean seemed louder than normal. And the lady with the big dog was getting closer.

"Uh, Donny, can I talk to you privately?" James pointed down the beach, the opposite way the woman was approaching.

"It's Dominic," he said, even though it didn't matter. He just needed to test his voice as his chest tightened and his mouth grew dry, but he didn't move.

James tapped a finger to where the gun was hidden beneath the hoodie, and as much as Dominic didn't want to put any distance between him and Carianna, keeping her safe was all that mattered.

He looked over his shoulder at her and the animation of her hands as she talked. John stared at her, listening, probably mesmerized by her. Maybe that would be enough for him not to cause her harm.

"Don't let him hurt her. I'll give you whatever you want," Dominic said when they stopped and were out of listening range.

"She your girlfriend?" James glanced at Dominic's hand, presumably for a ring, to see if maybe Carianna was his wife.

"Yes. And I love her very much." *Wow. How can I love her? But it feels like love.*

"Yeah, I'd like to love me some of that, for sure." James wiped his nose with his hand, grinning as he ogled Carianna. Dominic's blood boiled like a raging river of fury. But he didn't move or even breathe as the lady with the dog walked by them, far enough away, but too close for comfort. Dominic didn't want to drag anyone else into the scenario.

"All I have on me is my wallet. My credit cards are in there and about three hundred dollars in cash." He pointed to his back pocket. "Do you want me to get it?"

"Well, I'd be mighty obliged." James raised an eyebrow, his lopsided grin in full play.

Dominic hesitated. One quick kick would drop James to his knees, but as he glanced at Carianna, he ruled that out. John still had his hand on the knife. But he seemed entranced with whatever Carianna was saying, his head cocked to one side, an ear piqued in her direction.

Dominic handed James his wallet.

The thief pulled out the cash and counted as he flipped through five twenties and two hundred-dollar bills. He stuffed the cash into his front pocket and put the wallet in the back pocket of his jeans.

"Can we go now?" He considered asking for his driver's license, at the least, so he'd be able to board a plane, but he didn't want to do anything to prolong getting Carianna to safety.

James pushed back the head covering of his hoodie and scratched the top of his head, which was covered by a thick mop of dark hair. "Nah, not gonna be able to do that. My friend, John, has taken a liking to your pretty lady over there. We had somewhere important to be last night, but when she offered to meet us back here this morning, I reckon she must have taken a liking to John too. I think she'll be going with us." He lifted his hoodie for only a couple of seconds, flashing his weapon again. "So, we're gonna just walk away with her. And you're going to stay here."

Dominic realized at that moment that he'd led a fairly sheltered life. He'd never been in a situation even close to this. "That's not going to happen. You'll have to shoot me, and that will bring people flying out of those condos." He shakily nodded to his left. "Maybe just take the money and go."

James laughed out loud. "John's got a big knife on his hip, dude. Did you miss that?" He chuckled again.

"You think this is funny?" Dominic took a step toward James.

"Easy there, big fella." He held his palms facing Dominic.

Movement to Dominic's left caused him to turn and see Carianna walking towards him, and John was following quickly behind her.

Instinctively, Dominic walked towards her, and as a tear rolled down her face and her lip trembled, Dominic wrapped his arms around her.

"We have to go," she said in a shaky whisper. "Sometimes I'm wrong about people."

"Yes," he repeated. He eyed James while keeping one arm around Carianna. "We're leaving."

James looked at John, and they both smiled.

Two seconds later, James was plowed down into the sand by a loose Great Dane, who now lapped at his face like he was enjoying a giant lollypop.

"Oh my!" A woman wearing blue jeans, a white T-shirt, and white tennis shoes came running toward them. She had one hand on top of her head, holding down a floppy blue hat. "Jackson, you bad dog. Get off that man!" She stopped breathless in front of them, the dog still licking James, the weight of the animal pinning John into the sand.

Dominic moved closer to John when he saw John reaching for the knife, but Carianna put a hand on Dominic's arm and shook her head, as the woman struggled to get her dog off of James. It would have all been comical. But it wasn't.

"Jackson! Off of him!" She finally latched onto the dog's leash, and with John's help, the animal finally got off of James, who stood up, cursing like a sailor. "I'm so sorry!" The woman pointed a finger at the large animal. "Bad." Then she turned to Dominic. She was about the age his mother would have been, although Dominic's mother had been sick for so long, he barely remembered what she looked like prior to the cancer.

Carianna squatted down beside the dog and reached out her hand. The giant animal went to her and tucked his head into her chest as she scratched behind the dog's ears.

"He's just a big baby." The woman's brown hair was almost to her shoulders, but tucked behind her ears. She had a scar on her chin about two inches long. And deep. One eye seemed to have a mind of its own, drifting to the right every couple of seconds. "Sir, I'm sorry about that." She smiled, glancing at each of them.

Dominic wasn't sure when Carianna stood up or when his hand had found hers, but he had a firm hold as he glanced at everyone present. They could make a run for it, but that would leave the lady and her dog in danger.

"I'm so sorry to ask this." The woman pulled her hat tighter on her head and grimaced a little. "I see your picnic basket over there on the blanket. Is there any chance you might have some water? I forgot Jackson's water bottle, and he is incredibly thirsty. He got away from me, and I see he is still panting."

"He's beautiful," Carianna said. She was still joyfully scratching the dog behind the ears, as if they hadn't narrowly escaped a kidnapping and who knew what else. But now there were more players. James had his money. Maybe they would just take off.

Carianna stood up. Any hint of fear or nervousness was gone from her face. "I'll get Jackson some water. I have a full bottle in the picnic basket." She left the crowd, and Dominic drew in a deep breath, tempted to yell at her to run. But would James or John grab the lady with the dog? He slowly followed Carianna to the basket.

"Sorry again fellas," the woman said to John and James.

"Give me the water bottle, and then you run, as fast as you can, the way you did on the beach that day." Dominic whispered, but looked over his shoulder twice. The dog lady laughed, and John and James were smiling.

"No. It's okay." Carianna retrieved the water from the basket.

Dominic grabbed her arm, probably a little too hard because she flinched. "How can you say that? Just *run*."

Carianna nodded over Dominic's shoulder. "Look. They're leaving."

The lady waved at James and John, then made her way to Carianna and Dominic. She took the bottle of water Carianna offered her and started gently squirting water in Jackson's mouth. "Thank you so much," she said.

Dominic wondered if his knees would ever stop shaking. But as James and John strolled down the beach, he wondered what to do next. Go find the police before they attempted to harm someone else?

A voice in his head boomed. *They won't be harming anyone.* His eyes darted to Carianna, but she was busy packing up the blanket and other supplies. The dog lady was still giving Jackson water. Dominic heard the voice again. *They won't be harming anyone.* How could he be sure of that?

"My goodness, Jackson. You were thirstier than I thought." She straightened and held up the water bottle. "I'm afraid he drank all of your water."

"No worries." Carianna got right next to Dominic and put an arm around his waist. Just the feel of her calmed him.

"Well, I'm going to get going. I have an appointment with a friend for tea." She winked before she coaxed Jackson to start walking with her. "Oh." She stopped and reached into the back pocket of her jeans. "You must have lost this in the scuffle." She handed Dominic his wallet, and before Dominic could say anything, she was on her way down the beach with Jackson.

"She's an angel," Carianna said, smiling, as they watched the woman and her dog getting further down the beach.

"Yeah, she certainly came along at the right time." Dominic looked the opposite way, the direction John and James had gone. Nowhere in sight.

"No. She really *is* an angel." Carianna touched his arm, smiling.

Dominic reminded himself that Carianna believed she talked to God, so this shouldn't be surprising, but somehow it still was.

"I don't, uh, really believe that angels walk among us like that." Dominic opened his wallet. All his credit cards were there. And his cash. "I watched James put this money in his front pocket. How did it get back in my wallet?" He counted three hundred dollars, then put it back. Something glowed. He pulled out a wheat penny as he fought the urge to cry all of a sudden.

Carianna leaned up and kissed him on the cheek. "I bet you believe in angels now."

Dominic wasn't sure what he believed.

Chapter Eight

Carianna sat across the table from God, staying quiet. She knew He heard her thoughts, so sometimes there wasn't a need to say anything. But her heavenly Father finally spoke aloud.

"You're angry with me, Carianna."

"Yes." She set the china cup on the wooden table.

"Have I not always taken care of you? It is time for your father to join me in paradise. I know you will miss him, but he won't be sick anymore."

"I'm not prepared to say goodbye to him. And You haven't given me much warning."

God took a sip of tea, then said, "I felt it was your earthly father's place to tell you."

Carianna lowered her gaze, then looked up at him with tears in her eyes. "How long will Father be here?"

"Not long." God's eyes filled with water too. "But Carianna, I have never forsaken you, and I always have a plan for you."

Carianna shook her head. "I felt forsaken Saturday when those two bad men almost hurt me and Dominic. I reached out to You. You've never let anything like that happen to me, and I was afraid."

God nodded. "I know you were afraid. But Carianna, anger blocks My voice. You know that. We've talked about it. Burdens from the past, anger, resentment, and all the emotions you seldom have—those are things that keep people from hearing My voice. But I was there with you."

Carianna covered her face and sobbed. "I don't want to be afraid. And it scares me that Father will die." She looked up at God and swiped at her tears. "Is Dominic the man You sent to me?"

God smiled. "Yes."

"I liked him." She sniffled. "But he's gone. He cancelled our dinner that was scheduled for Sunday night, and he left on Tuesday. He's gone, and I haven't heard from him." Pausing, she shook her head. "I think You were wrong."

God picked up the gold and blue tea pitcher and filled Carianna's cup for exactly eight seconds. Her cup didn't overflow. It never did. He smiled a little. "I need you to trust me, Carianna."

Carianna swiped at her eyes as she fought to knock down the angry walls she'd constructed. She wasn't sure how she was going to function without Elijah in her life. And she'd thought something was happening with her and Dominic, but she'd been wrong about that too. But one thing was for sure. It would be impossible to function without God and His son Jesus, who had happened in on Thursdays more than once.

"I trust You," she said wearily.

"Go in peace, Carianna. I am with you."

She tried to smile, knowing God had never let her down. But she was still afraid.

Friday morning, Dominic took the second ferry to San Jose Island. He'd planned to be on the first one out, but he'd overslept.

He'd canceled his Tuesday flight, talked to his editor on the phone, ordered room service, and licked his wounds. He spent a large chunk of time reliving the scene on the beach, how close he and Carianna had possibly come to death, or at the least, extreme harm. And then he'd thought about the dog lady. He couldn't wrap his mind around what happened, and at first he'd continued to worry that James and John would venture down the beach, threatening someone else. Despite the voice he'd heard in his head—*they won't be harming anyone*—Dominic had eventually called the police and filed a report, giving a full description of the guys. He wasn't sure his faith or belief in angels was strong enough to risk Carianna's safety.

And he'd thought about Carianna. It had been six days since he'd seen or talked to her. He'd planned to walk away from her. But not without saying goodbye. He'd find her on the island, tell her how lovely it had been to spend time with her, and he'd catch a plane to Florida tomorrow. By now, surely her infatuation over him had simmered. Dominic wished he could feel the same. He was afraid he'd think of her for the rest of his life.

He looked around the ferry. Four passengers. Three older men toting large fishing rods and a woman, who looked close to Nanny's age, holding a smaller pole, with a bait bucket at her feet.

Dominic made the trek along the path that led to the beach. Two dolphins lifted their heads to his right, then disappeared. He spotted a huge turtle on one of the boulders underneath the water beside him. And when he finally rounded the corner and walked onto the beach, he scanned for as far as he could see. Carianna could be miles down the beach by now. He set out walking, describing Carianna to a few people he saw basking in the early morning sun or shell collecting. No one remembered seeing her. If she'd crossed anyone's path they would have seen the most beautiful woman in the world gliding by like an angel walking on clouds.

There weren't a lot of people on the beach. He passed two tents. Dominic had an adventuresome spirit, but perhaps he'd outgrown a tiny bit of it. He couldn't imagine camping on an island that had no running water, bathrooms, or any type of structure at all. He glanced at his cell phone in his hand. He had four bars. The island was close enough to a tower. At least the happy campers could have called for help in an emergency.

Two more ferries came and went, and no sign of Carianna.

By the time the last ferry pulled up to the dock, Dominic was sunburned, exhausted, hungry, and worried. Carianna had said she hadn't missed a Friday trip to San Jose Island in years. When he docked, he'd go to her house. He cringed thinking about having to face Millie. And did Carianna tell her father what almost happened to them on the beach?

Dominic followed three men as they loaded onto the last ferry. None of them were from the ferry this morning. Dominic was sure no one was stupid enough to stay on the island as long as he had.

As he took a seat near the back of the ferry, he recognized the crusty old guy from his first trip sitting a couple of feet to his right. He was digging through the knapsack.

"Find anything good today?" Dominic hoped the guy had found something spectacular, a rare find, even a chunk of gold or something. Because, at this point, there wasn't anything spectacular about the article he'd been working on. He'd lost interest somewhere in between falling in love with Carianna and almost getting killed.

The old guy shriveled his nose and frowned. Then he burst out laughing. "Ain't you ever heard of sunscreen, kid?"

Dominic scowled. "I didn't mean to be out there so long." He paused. "I was looking for Carianna. Did you see her today?"

Laughing, he said, "Still under her spell, eh?" He eyed Dominic long and hard, his mouth dropping into a frown. "It's Friday. She should have been there. She ain't ever missed a Friday that I can think of."

Dominic's stomach swirled with worry. And hunger. He pulled his sunglasses over his eyes as they neared the harbor.

"What are you still doing here anyway?" The old man closed his knapsack, but kept a hand on the bag. Maybe it was filled with gold? "I thought you'd be on to the next island by now."

"I will be. Tomorrow. But I've been spending time with Carianna." He peered at the man. "Her father isn't as scary as you made him out to be. But that crazy Nanny they live with is a piece of work." Dominic grunted, grinning, but when the old guy just stared at him with his eyebrows narrowed above his squinting eyes, Dominic added, "Yes, I've hung out at their house and even had dinner with them."

He didn't say anything for a few seconds. His heart skipped a beat when he recalled Elijah warning him not to get close to Carianna. And he'd done more than get closer to her. He loved her, as impossible as it seemed.

"I'm going to really miss Carianna when I leave." Just hearing the words stung like salt water in a wound. "But it's for the best."

The guy chuckled, then coughed, before spitting over the side of the boat, with barely enough time before the ferry rubbed against the wooden dock "Kid, you fell hard, didn't cha?"

"I guess so."

"So then. Just stay." He stood up, grabbing a pole to steady himself.

Dominic's jaw dropped.

"You heard me."

"Yeah, but after everything you said last time, I figured you to be the last person who would encourage me to stay." He paused as he stood up. "Carianna is special. No doubt." He edged closer to the man. "You've known her for her entire life, you said?" The man nodded. Dominic lowered her voice to barely above a whisper as the few passengers walked by him to exit the ferry. "Carianna believes she talks to God. I mean, like really talks to him. She has tea with him on—"

"Thursdays," the man interrupted.

Dominic closed his mouth and just stared at the old guy. "She also believes in angels, remembers when she born, and …" He lifted both shoulders before lowering them, sighing.

The old guy took a step closer to Dominic, his breath the briny smell of the ocean "You a Christian, boy?"

Dominic nodded. "Yes. I am."

"Then you pray, right?"

Sighing, Dominic hung his head for a few moments, thinking about how much he'd missed his mother. He hadn't really talked to God too often until he met Carianna. "I probably haven't been praying as much as I should, but yes…I pray."

"That's what Carianna is doing when she talks to God."

Dominic didn't move or say anything as the old guy got off the boat. But the man glanced over his shoulder, grinned, and then winked at Dominic, which seemed odd. It took his thoughts back to the lady with the dog on the beach.

His thoughts were interrupted when his flip-flop caught on a board on the floor of the ferry, just as he was about to step off he boat. He looked down. The man squatted down.

And he picked up the second wheat penny he'd found in the past decade or so.

Coincidence?

He stuffed it in his pocket, then jogged around the couple of people on the pier, and he picked up the pace until he got to his rental car in the parking lot. Squealing his tires, he drove as fast as he could to Carianna's house.

Something was wrong. He could feel it in his gut.

Chapter Nine

Dominic parked as close as he could get to Carianna's house, then ran all the way to the front door, passing a Closed sign on the door of the shop. He banged on the door repeatedly until Millie answered.

"Where's Carianna?" Breathing hard, he waited for Millie to hiss or stick her tongue out at him.

"Vacation." The old woman slammed the door in his face.

Dominic pounded on the door. "Millie! Open up!" He knocked continuously until she finally opened the door.

"Go away." She tried to close the door again, but Dominic slammed a hand to it before it closed.

"Where is Carianna? Is something wrong? Where is she?" He realized he was yelling when Millie cringed, then covered her ears for a couple of seconds. "Sorry. Where is she?"

Millie opened the door wide, leaning on her cane, wearing the same brown dress, dolphin earrings, and green Skechers. In the background were James and John. Every vein in Dominic's neck pulsated with tension as he fought a boxer's urge to lunge toward the men. He strained to see further into the living room, but he couldn't see around the corner where the couch was. "Where are Elijah and Carianna?" he asked in a whisper, pondering whether to make a run for it and get help. Would they shoot him? Harm Carianna or one of the others?

"Vacation." The old woman spoke between gritted teeth, but within seconds James was just over her shoulder.

"Hey, friend. Come on in." James smiled his crooked smile as he lay a hand on Nanny's shoulder, pressing down hard enough that the old woman groaned. "You weren't very convincing old lady. Now you've added another person to our party."

"I'm not your friend. Where is Carianna?" Dominic wasn't going to bow down to these guys. It was clear they weren't going away, and he had to question the voice he'd heard in his head, telling him that James and John weren't dangerous.

Dominic thought about just barreling into the room, but James thumped Millie on her back, again causing her to make a sound of discomfort, so Dominic hesitated and took a deep breath.

"Touch her again, and I'm coming over that threshold with everything I've got." Dominic's need to know that Carianna was okay drove his emotions. It might end up getting him killed, but he wasn't about to walk away.

James grinned, poking Millie again. But the old woman collapsed where she stood, melting into a puddle on the floor, her brown sack dress spreading around her like the witch in the Oz movie.

John came up behind James, a long knife in his hand. "What the …? Did you *kill* the old lady?"

"No! No, man. She just fainted or something." James pushed her with the tip of a worn black tennis shoe.

"Well, drag her inside." John pointed the knife at Dominic. "You get inside too."

Dominic thought he might vomit as he wondered how long they'd been here and what they might have done to Carianna and her father.

James grabbed one of Millie's arms and was about to drag her across the floor.

"Stop!" Dominic squatted down and scooped Millie into his arms. Then he followed James and John into the living room, his eyes scanning the room, landing on Carianna sitting on the couch beside her father. "Carianna. Are you okay?" She nodded, her face streaked with tears. Dominic locked eyes with

Elijah as the older man gargled and coughed. "Elijah?" Carianna's father didn't stop coughing, but he nodded.

Millie's arm dangled off to one side, and even though she didn't weigh much, Dominic was afraid he was going to drop her. "Can I least lay her on the bed?"

James nodded to John. "Follow him in the bedroom."

Dominic lay Millie on the Elijah's bed, checked her pulse, and asked John, "Can't I at least get her a drink of water or something?"

"No." He shoved Dominic back toward the living room.

God, where are you? Please help me get us out of this.

Carianna sat perfectly still with her hands folded in her lap. Elijah's bottom lip trembled in between more raspy coughs.

"It's going to be okay." Dominic scanned them both for injuries, but father and daughter appeared to be unharmed.

"Yeah. Everything is going to be just fine." John pulled the knife from its sheath, where he'd re-stashed it earlier, and as he moved toward Carianna, Dominic's pulse picked up even more. He was going to have to do something, no matter the risk. But just as he pondered what that might be, Millie let out a blood-curdling scream, followed by another one, even louder. Dominic started in that direction, but James shoved him, causing him to fall backward on the floor. Then there was a loud clunk and a body hitting the ground.

Dominic jumped to his feet and dove for James as he went for his gun, and this time he didn't hesitate to knee James where it would count. As James folded into a ball, Dominic got the gun and ran to the bedroom where he'd left Millie. The old lady breathed heavily as the weight of a lamp in her hand tipped her to one side. John was out cold on the floor, but Dominic could see him moving. He ran back to the living room. James was still in a fetal position. Carianna was crying. And Elijah was trying to tie James' hands behind his back with a phone cord he'd ripped from the wall. Dominic finished the job, then together they drug James back to the bedroom where John was, and once they had both men secure, Dominic held the gun pointed at them. He took a deep breath and pulled his cell phone from his pocket. In ragged, chopped sentences, he explained the situation as he fought to catch his breath and keep the pistol steady.

Carianna and Elijah took Millie to the kitchen to get her something to drink and to make sure she was okay. Dominic kept the gun on James and John, who was starting to wake up. It was a long five minutes before the police showed up and took statements from all of them, then they hauled James and John away in handcuffs.

Elijah and Millie sat down on the couch as Carianna rushed to Dominic. He held her at arm's length and looked her up and down. "You're sure you are okay?"

"Yes." She threw her arms around his neck, and Dominic held her close for a while, closing his eyes in a prayer of thanks. When he looked at Elijah and Millie, the exhaustion shone in both of their expressions.

It took about another hour for everyone to start feeling normal again, but Dominic suspected it would be a long time before they all weren't having nightmares about what could have happened.

After Dominic helped Carianna make them all a turkey sandwich for dinner, they attempted to eat, then retired to the living room with coffee. They were all quiet until Millie chuckled.

The old woman lifted her hands, palms out, fingers curved, ready to hiss at him again. Then she burst out laughing. "I thought for sure you'd run for the hills when I tried to trip you and stuck out my tongue." She chuckled again. "But you even stayed after I hissed at you." She shrugged. "I guess we'll keep you."

Dominic glanced at Carianna, who was smiling ear to ear.

It was exactly eight o'clock when Carianna walked onto the porch with Dominic. They gazed into each other's eyes, and Carianna struggled not to cry. "You're leaving tomorrow, right?"

Dominic tucked her hair behind her ears, then kissed her on the forehead, and Carianna knew what goodbye felt like, and the thought of him leaving sent a jolt of adrenaline shooting through her. But he had a life. A very different life than hers. *I am different too.*

"Yes, I'm scheduled to leave tomorrow." His eyes stayed on hers as she swallowed back a lump in her throat. "But what would you think if I stayed for a while? I could rent something a little more affordable than the condo I'm staying in." He shrugged. "And we can just see how it goes."

"What about your job and all the traveling you're supposed to do?" Her heart leapt at the prospect of him staying, but for how long?

"It just doesn't have the allure it used to." He smiled. "I have money that my mother left to me. I can afford to slow down and take the time to figure out what I want."

Carianna wanted to throw her arms around him. She wanted to tell him that she loved him, that God was right, that he is the one. But she pondered what he'd said for a few minutes, wondering if it would be selfish of her to encourage him to stay. "Why do you want to stay here, on Mustang Island?"

He grinned. "Why do you think?"

Father often called Carianna impetuous, but she threw her arms around Dominic, fighting the urge again to tell him that she loved him. Maybe he could feel her heart beating and somehow know it to be true. They held each other for a while before he eased her away.

"Something is bothering me." He sighed heavily. "That day on the beach, I was sure a voice in my head said to let those guys go, that they wouldn't harm anyone. I ended up reporting what happened anyway. But twice I heard that voice."

Carianna's heart hurt hearing this. "That's the *other* voice." She locked eyes with him. "The bad voice."

"How can you tell the difference?"

Carianna smiled. "Sometimes it's hard. The enemy is tricky."

Dominic nodded, then brought her hand to his lips and kissed it gently. "I don't really know how to pray, so I'm not surprised that it's hard for me to discern when it's the voice of God I hear." He paused, a troubled look on his face. "Or if it's someone else. At my mother's funeral, I heard a voice in my mind then too. The voice said I would find true love and be happy."

Carianna smiled. "That's the voice of God. Anything to do with love is God."

Dominic smiled. "I want to have a better relationship with God." He shrugged. "I'm not sure how to do that."

Now it was Carianna who brought his hand to her lips, kissing his fingers lightly. "I think I can help you with that." She closed her eyes and leaned her face against Dominic's chest, the feel of the Lord filling her heart, pushing away all ugly thoughts, relishing in her heavenly Father's love. *Thank you for Dominic, God.*

You are welcome sweet child of Mine.

Carianna's heart smiled, anxious to see what her future held.

Epilogue

Dominic hung the Closed sign in the window of the Shell Collector's shop, then pulled down the blind, darkening the room. He slipped out the door and walked the few steps to the house. As he crossed the threshold, Carianna had never looked more beautiful dressed in a white pair of Capri shorts, a pink sleeveless blouse, and white flip-flops. Her hair was pulled back into a high ponytail, and her mouth shimmered pink.

"Are you ready?" Dominic eyed the two suitcases beside her. The large brown one was his. Hers was a smaller red suitcase..

Carianna bounced up on her toes. "Yes!"

"Okay, I've got a bag with eight kolaches on the kitchen counter. Let's don't forget that." *Eight*. It represented infinity, the good in the universe, infinite love. Dominic had slipped into Carianna's world as easily as she'd stepped into his, and together they were building a life built on a solid foundation of faith, hope, and love.

After they married in March, Elijah had shown Carianna and Dominic how to make his kolaches, much to Millie's horror. She'd been trying to get the family recipe for years. Elijah had been a proud father walking his daughter down the aisle of the small church they attended in town. But his health deteriorated fast after that, and Carianna and Dominic were by his side when he passed. They'd laid him to rest in the church cemetery, and they visited him often.

Dominic was sure that he and Carianna had stumbled into each other's life as part of God's grand plan for them. Carianna continued to have tea with God on Thursdays, and Dominic didn't question it. He'd learned that everyone has a special way of communicating with our heavenly Father. There wasn't really a right or a wrong way, just a sincere desire to seek Him in all we do. Carianna's patience with Dominic as he found his spiritual footing led him to find peace about his mother. He was also learning to discern the voices in his head, and mostly he just loved the life that God had gifted him.

Millie walked into the living area from her room in the back of the house, munching on a carrot, those two front teeth hard at work, and it took everything

Dominic had not to laugh. But he'd grown fond of the old woman. She made him laugh, and the older lady would do anything for him and Carianna.

"Millie…" Dominic had called her Nanny to her face one time, and she'd quickly set him straight about it. He tried not to make the mistake again. "All your medications are lined out on that big calendar I bought you, and they are in that container marked with each day of the week. We'll be gone eight days, and Sherry from two doors down will be checking on you. Carol will open the shop for a few hours a day in the afternoon while we're gone, and I've posted those temporary hours on the door."

Millie leaned on her cane, squinted her eyes at him, and said. "You worry too much."

He grinned. "Not nearly as much as I used to."

The community had slowly come to accept Dominic as Carianna's husband, although he was sure that male hearts were broken all over he island. But he and Carianna were successfully running her father's shop and blissfully happy.

He turned to his beautiful wife who had changed his life more than he could have imagined.

"You ready?" He picked up both of the suitcases while Carianna ran to get the bag of kolaches.

She nodded. "Yep! Off to the Grand Canyon." She gave Millie a long, but gentle hug.

Millie put up her paws and hissed at Dominic, which always made her snort with laughter afterwards.

Then he stood beside his wife, and they took eight carefully measured steps to the door, both their hearts filled to capacity with love.

Thank you, Lord.

Grab another novella in the Surf's Up series!

AVAILABLE NOW!

Addison and Logan aren't in the market for love. She's recovering from a breakup, and he is hiding out on Galveston Island, trying to save enough money to get back to his country of origin before his world crashes down around him. But when Addison awakens feelings in him that he thought died long ago, Logan begins to question whether or not fleeing from the past is worth leaving Addison forever.

Can love triumph where currents are rough?

Turn the page for a sample!

Chapter One

Addison paced across her mother's living room as sweat dampened her temples and the base of her neck. May was already punishing them with Texas temperatures that were usually reserved for July and August. But Lee Ann Burke had a steadfast rule not to run the air conditioning until July. If there was any saving grace at all, it was the ocean pushing a breeze ashore, which wafted through the screened windows of the house Addison had grown up in. She breathed in the briny aroma, a smell she'd haul to her grave someday, with enough good and bad memories to keep her balanced on the plank she'd been walking since her father died.

She glanced at her smartphone, wondering if she was going to make it to her next appointment on time. The continuous drip of the kitchen faucet around the corner felt like water torture against her left temple. She rubbed the source of the irritation. "Mom, are you sure the agency said three o'clock? It's almost three thirty."

"That's what they said." Her mother didn't glance up, but kept focused on the jigsaw puzzle she was hunched over. Addison couldn't recall a time that her family—small as it was—had ever shared a meal at the kitchen table, except maybe Christmas and Thanksgiving. On most days, her mother had one of her puzzles spread atop the oak table, with a sweating glass of sweet tea nearby and an ashtray. There was still sweat tea within reach, but at least Mom had taken to smoking her cigarettes outside a few years ago, something she should have done when it became common knowledge that secondhand smoke was unhealthy. Addison recalled all the smoke she and her father had inhaled over the years, wondering if that might have contributed to her father's cancer diagnosis. Addison could still smell the stench of tobacco in the house. In light of recent events, she wondered if her mother would quit smoking. *Doubtful.* If she didn't quit after they found out Dad had cancer, Addison doubted she'd do it now.

Addison glanced at the TV trays in the stand next to the couch, the rust barely visible amidst the flowery design that vined up the legs and covered the tops. She couldn't help but smile. Some of her happiest moments were in this living room eating on

TV trays and watching "Everyone Loves Raymond." Her father had loved that show, and sometimes Addison could almost hear her father's laughter late at night, right before she drifted off to sleep. Maybe he was sending her a message that she'd laugh again one day too.

Sighing, she walked to the window to get the full effect of the breeze, and after another twenty minutes of pacing the living room, she was glad to see a car turning in the driveway. "Mom, the caregiver from the agency is here." She turned to face her mother, who still didn't look up. "Mom, did you hear me?"

Slowly, her mother pulled her eyes up until they were locked with Addison's. "I had a stroke, Addie, I'm not deaf." Scowling, she looked back at her puzzle, then mumbled, "And I don't need a babysitter."

Addison shook her head, feeling a trickle of perspiration roll down her face. They'd had this conversation a dozen times, at least. "I know you don't need a babysitter, and this woman isn't being hired for that. She's just here for a few weeks, to make sure you don't fall again and to help around the house. Just until you get your strength back."

When her mother didn't respond, Addison wound around the coffee table and moved toward the front door, surprised to see a man standing on the other side of the screen. "Can I help you?"

"G'day. I'm Logan Northrupp. The agency sent me to..." He unfolded a piece of paper, scanned it, then looked at Addison. "This is 222 Beachfront Drive, right? I'm here to take care of Lee Ann Burke."

It took Addison a few seconds to realize he'd said "good day." It sounded like "goodie." Addison didn't say anything for a few moments, even though she heard a slight chuckle from her mother. "Uh... I guess I just assumed they were sending a woman."

Mom cleared her throat. "To assume is to make an—"

"Mother!" Addison peered over her shoulder. "Stop." Mom shrugged, and Addison turned back to the tall man still on the other side of the door. She eased the door open and stepped aside. "Sorry it's so hot in here."

"No problem." He smiled, and Addison tried to identify his accent, which made him even better looking than he already was. Wavy blond hair, parted in the middle, hung to the collar of his white golf shirt, which sported an emblem with the agency's logo. Logan looked more like a lifeguard than a caregiver, she thought as she eyed his chiseled arms, golden tan, and eyes as deep blue as the ocean. Her eyes cut to his left hand. No ring. There was a time in her life when Addison would have latched on to such beauty. But usually, when a single man pushing thirty looks this good, there is something wrong with him.

A truckload of baggage, perhaps. Maybe a criminal record, although doubtful since he was hired out by an agency. Maybe he just wasn't a nice person. *Or gay.*

She motioned toward her mother at the table. "This is my mother, Lee Ann Burke." She paused. "Mom, this is Logan from the agency."

"Nice to meet you, Mrs. Burke."

Addison's mother finished fitting a piece of the puzzle, then stood up, and hobbled toward Addison and Logan on shaky legs, stopping a few feet short of Logan. "Addie believes that I have one foot in the grave, but not only am I not planning to check out just yet, but I'm also not old enough to be called Mrs. Burke. Please just call me Lee Ann." Mom extended her hand to Logan, and while Addison cringed at her mother's idea of an introduction, it could have gone much worse.

"Then Lee Ann it is." He smiled again, flashing a set of pearly whites, then offered Addison the file folder he was holding. "This details my credentials, and there is also a list of duties that the agency gave me, if you'd like to look over it to make sure there isn't something else you'd like me to do during my time here."

Addison looked over the paperwork. He'd been a caregiver for almost two years. Not much experience, but then Addison's mother wasn't going to require much. Logan would be more of a babysitter, as Mom had said. Addison was worried her mother's mind had suffered, and the doctor said her likelihood of having another stroke was highest over the next couple of months. Even before the stroke, Mom often forgot to take her blood pressure meds.

"It says under the list of duties that you'll be here from ten in the morning until three in the afternoon, and that's fine. But it also says that you'll prepare a home-cooked meal each day for Mom's lunch." Addison glanced up at him. "She's shaky on her legs from a recent fall, but she can make her own lunch, a sandwich or something."

Smiling again, he said, "I'm a chef, so I just offered that on my own."

Addison chewed on her bottom lip in an effort not to propose to the guy here and now. *Baggage or not.*

"Hello, I'm right here," her mother interjected. "Had a stroke. Not deaf, remember?" She cleared her throat, raising her chin a bit. Mom was an attractive woman who didn't look her sixty-two years, which was surprising considering the smoking, lack of exercise, and two stiff whiskey sours each night. Addison held her breath as she waited for her mother to go on. "Logan, I think it would be lovely if you prepared us lunch every day, and I'd be happy to pay for anything you need in the way of groceries to do so." Mom moved slowly toward the front door, looking over her shoulder once. "You kids work out the details while I have a smoke. But I wouldn't be opposed to a sponge bath, if you'd like to put that on the agenda." She giggled as the screen slammed behind her.

Available now on Amazon!

Also available in the Surf's Up series!

One man. Two women. A child desperate for medical treatment. How can Kyle choose between the woman he once loved and his current fiancée? Is there a solution that suits all involved, or will someone end up out of the triangle forever?

Kyle loses the love of his life when girlfriend, Morgan is whisked away by the CIA in the middle of the night. Almost six years later, two men show up at Kyle's door with news that he has a daughter who is ill. Her only chance of survival lies with Kyle, if he'll fly to an undisclosed island location in the pacific. But reuniting with his first love and saving his daughter places his engagement to his fiancée, Lexie, at risk.

Can love bridge the troubled waters of Kyle's past and present?

Turn the page for a sample!

Prologue

Kyle stretched tape across another box, then lifted it from the floor and piled it on top of the others that he had ready to go.

"I can't believe all this stuff was stashed in this small room." Lexie lowered a stack of file folders into a box. "I don't think I had nearly this much in my dorm room." She grinned as she slung long brown hair over her shoulders. "And I'm a girl. We keep everything."

Kyle eyed the organized mess in the place he'd called home over the past four years. "Some of it probably needs to be trashed, but I'll take a closer look at everything once I get settled in my apartment." He handed Lexie the tape. "Just think, you'll be right downstairs from me. No curfews or rules. We can eat pizza at three in the morning, and we won't have to deal with crazy roommates."

Lexie closed the distance between them and pressed her soft lips gently against his. Kyle eased his arms around her and basked in the scent of her flowery perfume. The feel of her mouth on his was a welcome distraction. They'd briefly considered moving in together, but Kyle's Catholic upbringing kept him from choosing that option. They'd done the next best thing: rented apartments close to each other.

"Maybe we should take a break from packing," Kyle whispered in her ear, trailing kisses down her neck.

She wiggled out of his arms. "Behave. We've got to get this done. You've got to be out of here by the end of the day." She walked to the built-in drawers in Kyle's room and tugged the bottom one until it inched open. "Good grief. What is all this?"

Kyle shuffled across the floor in his socks until he was beside her and staring at the massive amount of pictures, ticket stubs, receipts, and other memorabilia crammed in the top drawer. Sighing, he thumbed his way through the first layer. "Keepsakes."

Lexie smiled as she picked up a picture. "Awe, look at you and Aiden. So handsome."

"My mom sent me that the first week I was here, along with a bunch of other pictures." Kyle recalled how homesick he was at that time. "I was probably seventeen in that picture. Aiden was sixteen."

"Baseball players, I see." Lexie brought the photo closer to her face. "You and your brother look a lot alike in this picture, but not so much in person." She reached for a ticket stub that was folded in half and straightened it. Kyle rolled his eyes as she burst out laughing. "Lady Gaga?"

Kyle shrugged as his mind flooded with memories. "Yeah, well. I wasn't the one who wanted to go see her, but she actually put on a great show."

"Was this your date?" Lexie held up a photo that was right underneath the ticket. Kyle had his arm around the first girl he'd ever loved. Morgan Calhoun. And thoughts of her still caused his heart to race, even though he was sure no one could be in love as much as he and Lexie. There was no doubt in his mind that he'd marry Lexie one day.

"Yeah. That's Morgan." He swallowed hard. "We grew up on the same street, our families went to the same church, and our moms were best friends." He forced a smile. "My first—and only love—before you."

"Kyle Brossmann, do you expect me to believe that there have only been two loves in your life?"

The question made Kyle wonder how many loves had been in Lexie's life, but it really didn't matter. He'd be the one blessed to live with her for the rest of his days. He hoped.

Kyle nodded. "Yep. There was Morgan. And now you." He eased the photo from her hand and studied

Morgan's face, the way her blonde hair curled under slightly below her chin, then tapered past her shoulders. She had magnificent brown eyes and a smile that made people like her before she ever uttered a word. And a body that made guys go nuts. Kyle had questioned her interest in him from day one, knowing someone as attractive as Morgan could have dated anyone she wanted.

"She's really pretty. I'm surprised you haven't mentioned her before." Lexie put her head on his shoulder. "How long did you two date?"

Kyle tucked his dark hair behind his ears, knowing he'd have to shed his long locks before he started his new job. "We dated about a year, but we sort of grew into it. Since we'd known each other most of our lives, we were friends way before anything else." He set the picture back in the drawer, forcing thoughts of Morgan away. Five years later, it was still painful to think about her. But Lexie had already found another selfie of Morgan and Kyle at the beach, the murky Gulf of Mexico in the background. Kyle remembered the cloudy day in Galveston. They'd eaten at Shrimp 'N Stuff and walked on the beach. Kyle looked like his face was twice as big as it really was in the picture. But Morgan looked perfect in her pink bikini top and freshly applied lip gloss.

Lexie couldn't seem to pull her eyes away from the photo. That's the affect Morgan had on most people.

"So what happened with you two?"

It was a conversation Kyle didn't want to have, but if he was going to marry Lexie some day, he supposed there shouldn't be any secrets. "It's a crazy story."

Lexie nudged him gently with her elbow, grinning. "I love crazy stories."

Kyle took a deep breath as all the memories he'd fought to suppress came rushing to the surface. He lowered himself to the edge of the mattress, perching on the corner as he began. "Back in high school, I pulled up to Morgan's house in my truck and honked the horn. She rode with me to school every day, even though she had her own car. I waited, honked again, waited some more, then finally went to the front door and knocked. No answer." His heart hammered against his chest, but he figured he might as well get this over with, then he'd pack up his memories for good. Seal them tight with extra tape, keepsakes his grandchildren would find some day and ask, "Who is this woman grandpa is with?" From heaven, he'd whisper, "My first love."

"Then what?" Lexie eased her way to the bed and sat down.

"I looked in the window, and through the sheer drapes, I could see that the living room was empty. I mean, totally empty. No furniture. Nothing." Kyle felt the sweat beads pooling on his forehead, much like five years ago. "I opened the front door, which was unlocked, and I went through the whole house yelling Morgan's name." He turned to face Lexie, pushed the drawer shut with the heel of one foot, then leaned against the dresser. "There was not one piece of furniture in that entire house."

"I'm confused." Lexie tipped her head to one side, frowning. "Did Morgan and her family just pack up in the middle of the night and disappear?"

Kyle tried to calm the churning in his stomach. "That's exactly what happened."

"Where'd they go?"

"No one knows. It was totally bizarre."

Available now on Amazon!

Other books by Beth Wiseman

The Daughters of the Promise series (Amish)
Plain Perfect   *Plain Paradise*
Plain Pursuit   *Plain Proposal*
Plain Promise   *Plain Peace*

Land of Canaan series (Amish)
Seek Me With All Your Heart
The Wonder of Your Love
His Love Endures Forever

Amish Secrets series
Her Brother's Keeper
Love Bears All Things
Home All Along

Women's Fiction
Need You Now
The House that Love Built
The Promise

Surf's Up Novellas
A Tide Worth Turning
Message In A Bottle
The Shell Collector's Daughter

Surf's Up Short Story
Christmas by the Sea

About the Author

Beth Wiseman is the best-selling author of the Daughters of the Promise series and the Land of Canaan series. Having sold almost two million books, her novels have held spots on the ECPA (Evangelical Christian Publishers Association) Bestseller List and the CBA (Christian Book Association) Bestseller List. She was the recipient of the prestigious Carol Award in 2011 and 2013.

She is a three-time winner of the Inspirational Readers Choice Award, and an INSPY Award winner. In 2013 she took home the coveted Holt Medallion. Her first book in the Land of Canaan series—*Seek Me With All Your Heart*—was selected as the 2011 Women of Faith Book of the Year. Beth and her husband are empty nesters enjoying country life in South Central Texas.

Visit **BethWiseman.com** to subscribe to Beth's newsletter. Subscribers enjoy cover reveals, bonus material, free downloads, and exclusive news about future releases. Beth only sends one newsletter per month. Visit Beth at **Fans of Beth Wiseman on Facebook** where she interacts with readers and shares about her writing life.

CPSIA information can be obtained
at www.ICGtesting.com
Printed in the USA
LVOW13s1916160517
534728LV00010B/472/P